THE
GHOST
RIDER

Born in 1936, Ismail Kadare is Albania's best-known poet and novelist. Translations of his novels have appeared in more than forty countries. In 2005 he was awarded the first Man Booker International Prize for 'a body of work written by an author who has had a truly global impact'. He is the recipient of the highly prestigious 2009 Principe de Asturias de las Lettras in Spain.

Also by Ismail Kadare

The General of the Dead Army
The Wedding
Broken April
The Concert
The Palace of Dreams
The Three-Arched Bridge
The Pyramid
The File on H
Albanian Spring: Anatomy of Tyranny
Elegy for Kosovo
Spring Flowers, Spring Frost

Published by Canongate
The Successor
Chronicle in Stone
Agamemnon's Daughter, with The Blinding Order
and The Great Wall
The Siege
The Accident

THE
GHOST
RIDER

ISMAIL KADARE

Translated from the French of Jusuf Vrioni by Jon Rothschild
Updated, with new sections added, by Ismail Kadare
and David Bellos

Introduction by David Bellos

CANONGATE
Edinburgh · London · New York · Melbourne

Published by Canongate Books in 2010

1

First published as *Kush i solli Doruntinen?* in 1980 in the collection
Gjakftohtësia by Naim Frashëri, Tirana

First English edition published as *Doruntine* in 1988 by New Amsterdam
Books, 4720 Boston Way, Lanham, MD 20706 and by Saqi Books, London

This edition first published as *The Ghost Rider* in Great Britain in 2010 by
Canongate Books Ltd, 14 High Street, Edinburgh EH1 1TE

www.meetatthegate.com

British Library Cataloguing-in-Publication Data
A catalogue record for this book is available on
request from the British Library

ISBN 978 1 84767 341 1

Typeset in Goudy by Palimpsest Book Production Ltd,
Grangemouth, Stirlingshire

Printed and bound in Great Britain by Clays Ltd, St Ives plc

INTRODUCTION

"Have you ever read Bürger's *Lenore?*" asks the narrator of Ismail Kadare's *Twilight of the Gods of the Steppes*, as he wanders along a beach with a girl, at a writers' retreat in Soviet Latvia. "Or Zhukovski's *Ludmilla?* It's the same story, you know. He translated it from Bürger."

"So who did Bürger steal it from?" the young woman asks.

"I opened my mouth to say 'From us!' but managed to stop in time so as not to put myself in the position of those representatives of small nations ever eager to say 'we, our people, in our land . . .' with a kind of pride or bombast that I found depressing because it always struck me that they didn't believe what they were saying either."

The story in question is "The Ballad of Constantine and Doruntine", an ancient tale that is known wherever Albanian is spoken – within the current borders of the state, among the Arberësh of southern Italy, in Kosova, Montenegro and Macedonia. Versions of it exist in every Balkan language and in several other European folk traditions. It was put into verse (and liberally altered) by the German Romantic poet Gottfried August Bürger (1748–1794) in the famous ballad "Lenore", which is where Edgar Allan Poe probably found the name that he used in his own dirge, "Lenore". Known in folklore studies as the "Lenore motif", the legend tells of a brother (Constantine, or Kostandin in Albanian) who rises from his grave to fulfil his promise of bringing his married sister Doruntine back from a far-off land to see their dying mother. *The Ghost Rider* tells the same story from an unconventional perspective – that of the detective whose task it is to unravel what really happened.

Like the legend of Rozafat – the bridge made safe by walling up a living victim inside it, developed most fully in *The Three-Arched Bridge* and recalled, from a great distance, in *The Great Wall* – the story of Kostandin and Doruntine is a recurring motif in Ismail Kadare's vast œuvre. *The Ghost Rider* is Kadare's fullest exploitation of what might first seem just a Gothic treasure of Albanian national folklore, save that Kadare is reluctant from the start, as the passage from his early novel of life in the Soviet Union suggests, to cast himself or his narrator as a "representative of a small nation ever eager to say 'we, our people, in our land . . .'" He would rather see himself as a representative of literature, a messenger from a broad, deep and mysterious place, telling stories that echo far beyond the boundaries of any one land.

The Twilight of the Gods of the Steppes was first drafted shortly after Albania broke off relations with the Soviet Union in 1960. *The Ghost Rider* was written fifteen years later, after Albania broke off relations with the People's

Republic of China, and thus found itself once again radically isolated – a tiny nation a few hours' boat ride from Bari but a million miles from the concert of nations in the economic, cultural and political spheres. For Kadare, the Lenore motif rises up from the deep memory of national folklore at times when relations with the outside world are cut off. In the 1960s, Soviet–Albanian couples must have found themselves in situations reminiscent of Doruntine's, if not of Kostandin's. It may be especially significant that for his major treatment of the theme he uses a version of the ballad coming not from Albania proper, but from the Arbëresh tradition of southern Italy. "Marrying out", even into the Albanian-speaking communities of nearby Sicily, was quite unthinkable at that time. Folktale and fiction allow Kadare to take a subtly contrary path that thinks the unthinkable without seeming to deal with present issues at all.

Kadare's own position in the later 1970s was not an easy one. Translations of his work had been appearing in Paris since 1970 and he was now widely known in the West. That gave him a degree of protection, but at the same time made him especially vulnerable to accusations of collusion with the enemy – for why would bourgeois readers praise him so highly unless his novels were somehow speaking to bourgeois interests? Subjected to public anathema and to an excruciating self-criticism session at the Writers' Union over his poem "The Red Pashas" in 1975, he was subsequently rusticated to the provincial city of Berat for the best part of a year, and banned from publishing novels for an indeterminate period (despite being at the same time an appointed member of the People's

Assembly). For that reason, Kadare's novels of the later 1970s – which in retrospect can be seen as the most creative period in his life – were disguised as short stories; several of them, including *Broken April* and *The Ghost Rider*, were published in a collection entitled *Cold Blood* in 1980.

During this period, Kadare's works were regularly translated into French inside Albania by his long-standing collaborator, Jusuf Vrioni, and his retelling of the Ballad of Constantine was brought out by Fayard in 1986 as *Qui a ramené Doruntine?*, a literal translation of the Albanian title. It came into English much more quickly than most of Kadare's works, translated from Vrioni's French by Jon Rothschild in 1988, as *Doruntine*. Over the following twenty years, the paranoid Stalinist regime of Enver Hoxha collapsed and disappeared, Ismail Kadare moved to Paris and, once there, undertook to republish his complete works in matching volumes in Albanian and French, organised by the historical periods of the novels' action. *The Ghost Rider*, set in a generic Middle Ages, (preceded only by *The Pyramid*, set in Ancient Egypt, and short stories set in the mythological or classical past) was therefore included in Volume 1, published in 1993, in a significantly reworked and expanded version.

The revisions made by Kadare are essentially of an artistic nature – replacing brief generalities with additional narrative, including a few new named characters, or else expanding dialogues to give a fuller sense of the issues at stake – but they also include the restoration of historical and political references it would have been unwise to include during the Hoxha regime, notably to religious practices and, in this novel, to discussions that imply the possibility of disagreement with state authority. Even so, it requires a leap of our imaginations to read in the character of Kostandin, as he is recalled by his comrades in chapters six and seven, a figure of resistance and dissidence. Yet that is what he is, and also what makes him unique in Kadare's universe, which usually suggests the human values that it promotes by antiphrasis, understatement and what another critic has called the device of "distant echo".

The medieval setting of *The Ghost Rider* is never precisely dated in the legend, but Kadare took care to connect his version of the story to the general history of his country. Albania occupies an area that was formerly the Roman province of Illyria, and it was Christianised very early on. When the Roman Empire divided in 378 AD, Albania was assimilated into the Eastern Empire based on Constantinople (Byzantium), but when the churches of Rome and Byzantium divided in the eleventh century, the Albanian lands remained predominantly Catholic. The area was frequently raided and partly colonised in turn by Bulgars, Serbs, Venetians and Norman knights, and between the eleventh and fourteenth centuries it found itself at the wavering frontier between Roman Catholicism and the Eastern Church. Out of these turbulent times, and pending the greater conflict between the Ottomans and the European powers which would see Albania absorbed into the Muslim world for many centuries, a nation that at that time called itself Arbëria was slowly emerging.

The Ghost Rider relates the legend of Doruntine to the invention or emergence of the *besa*, the Albanian "promise" or "troth" from which the rules of hospitality and the blood feud are derived in the fifteenth-century Kanun of Lek Dukagjin, the famous and long-lasting code of Albanian customary law. But alongside his speculation on the origins of a key part of Albanian national identity – a part that Enver Hoxha, self-proclaimed "engineer of human souls", was seeking to eradicate and replace with the "New Man" – Kadare uses the legend to broach more pressing and dangerous questions: What are the means of resistance that a culture can use when under attack? How do people organise themselves to survive oppression? It is not a coincidence that the police chief charged with elucidating the mystery of Doruntine's return in Kadare's novel often sounds like a harassed bureaucrat of modern times trying hard to hang on to rationality when all around him seem to have gone mad.

For this new edition of Jon Rothschild's original translation, I have inserted the many additions made by Kadare in 1993, and also put personal and place names in forms closer to their Albanian originals. In addition, Ismail Kadare has authorised one or two further small changes that improve the coherence of the text, as well as the new title.

David Bellos
Princeton, NJ, May 2009

GUIDE TO PRONUNCIATION

Most letters of the Albanian alphabet are pronounced more or less as in English. The main exceptions are as follow:

c	*ts* as in cur*ts*y
ç	*ch* as in *ch*urch
gj	*gy* as in ho*gy*ard
j	*y* as in *y*ear
q	*ky* as in stoc*ky*ard or the *t* in mature
x	*dz* as in a*dz*e
xh	*j* as in *j*oke
zh	*s* as in measure

CHAPTER ONE

Stres was still in bed when he heard the knocking at the door. He was tempted to bury his head in the pillow to blot out the noise, but the sound came again, louder this time.

"Who the Devil would pound on my door before daybreak?" he grumbled, throwing off the blanket.

He was on his way down the stairs when he heard the hammering for the third time, but now the rhythm of the metal knocker told him who it was. He slid back the bolt and opened the door. There was no need to say, "And what possesses you to wake me before dawn?" for the look on his face and his bleary eyes conveyed the message well enough.

"Something's happened," his deputy hastened to say.

Stres stared at him sceptically, as if to say, "It better be good to justify a visit at this ungodly hour." But he was well aware that his aide rarely blundered. Indeed, whenever he had been moved to rebuke him, he had found himself compelled to hold his tongue. Still, he would have been delighted had his deputy been in the wrong this time, so that he could work off his ill humour on him.

"So?"

The deputy glanced at his chief's eyes for an instant, then stepped back and spoke.

"The dowager Vranaj and her daughter, Doruntine, who arrived last night under very mysterious circumstances, both lie dying."

"Doruntine?" said Stres, dumbfounded. "How can it be?"

His deputy heaved a sigh of relief: he had been right to pound on the door.

"How can it be?" Stres said again, rubbing his eyes as if to wipe away the last trace of sleep. And in fact he had slept badly. No first night home after a two-week mission had ever been so trying. One long nightmare. "How can it be?" he asked for the third time. Doruntine had married into a family that lived so far from her own that she hadn't been able to come back even when they were in mourning.

"How, indeed," said the deputy. "As I said, the circumstances of her return are most mysterious."

"And?"

"Well, both mother and daughter have taken to their beds and lie dying."

"Strange! Do you think there's been foul play?"

The deputy shook his head. "I think not. It looks more like the effect of some dreadful shock."

"Have you seen them?"

"Yes. They're both delirious, or close to it. The mother

keeps asking, 'Who brought you back, daughter?' And the daughter keeps saying, 'My brother Kostandin.'"

"Is that what she says: Kostandin? But, good God, he died three years ago, he and all his brothers . . ."

"According to the local women now gathered at their bedsides, that is just what the mother told her. But the girl insists that she arrived with him last night, just after midnight."

"How odd," said Stres, all the while thinking how *ghastly*.

They stared at each other in silence until Stres, shivering, remembered that he was not dressed.

"Wait for me," he said, and went back in.

From inside came his wife's drowsy "What is it?" and the inaudible words of his reply. Soon he came out again, wearing the regional captain's uniform that made him look even taller and thinner.

"Let's go see them," he said.

They set out in silence. A handful of white rose petals fallen at someone's door reminded Stres somehow of a brief scene from the dream that had slipped so strangely into his fitful sleep.

"Quite extraordinary," he said.

"It beggars belief," replied his deputy, raising the stakes.

"To tell you the truth, I was tempted not to believe it at first."

"So I noticed. It's unbelievable, isn't it. Very mysterious."

"Worse than that," Stres said. "The more I think about it, the more inconceivable it seems."

"The main thing is to find out how Doruntine got back," said the deputy.

"And then?"

"The case will be solved if we can find out who accompanied her, or rather, if we can uncover the circumstances of her arrival."

"Who accompanied her," Stres repeated. "Yes, who and how . . . Obviously she is not telling the truth."

"I asked her three times how she got here, but she offered no explanation. She was hiding something."

"Did she know that all her brothers, including Kostandin, were dead?" Stres asked.

"I don't know. I don't think so."

"It's possible she didn't know," Stres said. "She married so far away . . ." To his surprise his jaw suddenly felt as heavy as lead, making it difficult for him to speak. What's wrong with me? he wondered. He could feel a heaviness in his lungs too, as if they had filled with coal dust.

He pressed forward, and the exercise helped to clear his dulled mind.

"What was I saying? Oh, yes . . . She married so far abroad that she's not been able to return home since her wedding. As far as I know this is the first time she's been back."

"She can't have known about the death of her nine brothers or she would have come then," said the deputy. "The dowager complained often enough about her daughter not being at her side during those grief-stricken days."

"The forests of Bohemia where she lives lie at least

two weeks' journey from here, if not more," Stres observed.

"Yes, if not more," repeated his deputy. "Almost at the heart of Europe."

As they walked, Stres noticed more white rose petals strewn along the path, as if some invisible hand had scattered them during the night. Fleetingly he recalled seeing them somewhere before. But he couldn't really remember his dream. He also had a faint pain in his forehead. At the exact spot where his dream must have entered last night, he thought, before exiting the same way later on, towards dawn perhaps, irritating the wound it had already made.

"In any event, someone must have come with her," he said.

"Yes, but who? Her mother can't possibly believe that her daughter returned with a dead man, any more than we can."

"But why would she conceal who she came back with?"

"I can't explain it. It's very unclear."

Once again they walked in silence. The autumn air was cold. Some cawing crows flew low. Stres watched their flight for a moment.

"It's going to rain," he said. "The crows caw like that because their ears hurt when a storm is coming."

His deputy looked off in the same direction, but said nothing.

"Earlier you mentioned something about a shock that might have brought the two women to their deathbed," Stres said.

"Well, it was certainly caused by some very powerful emotion." He avoided the word *terrible*, for his chief had commented that he tended to overuse it. "Since neither woman shows any mark of violence, their sudden collapse must surely have been caused by some kind of shock."

"Do you think the mother suddenly discovered something terrible?" Stres asked.

His deputy stared at him. He can use words as he pleases, he thought in a flash, but if others do, he stuffs them back down their throats.

"The mother?" he said. "I suspect they both suddenly discovered something terrible, as you put it. At the same time."

As they continued to speculate about the shock mother and daughter had presumably inflicted on one another (both Stres and his deputy, warped by professional habit, increasingly tended to turns of phrase better suited to an investigative report), they mentally reconstructed, more or less, the scene that must have unfolded in the middle of the night. Knocks had sounded at the door of the old house at an unusual hour, and when the old lady called out – as she must have done – "Who's there?" – a voice from outside would have answered, "It's me, Doruntine." Before opening the door, the old woman, upset by the sudden knocking and convinced that it couldn't be her daughter's voice, must have asked, to ease her doubt, "Who brought you back?" Let us not forget that for three years she had been desperate for some consolation in her grief, waiting in vain for her daughter to come home. From outside, Doruntine answered, "My brother Kostandin brought me back." And the old woman receives the first shock. Perhaps, even shaken as she was, she found the strength to reply, "What are you talking about? Kostandin and his brothers have been in their graves for three years." Now it is Doruntine's turn to be stricken. If she really believes that it was her brother Kostandin who had brought her back, then the shock is twofold: finding out that Kostandin and her other brothers were dead and realising at the same time that she had been travelling with a ghost. The old woman then summons up the strength to open the door, hoping against hope that she has misunderstood the young woman's words, or that she has been hearing voices, or that it is not Doruntine at the door after all. Perhaps Doruntine, standing there outside, also hopes she has misunderstood. But when the door swings open, both repeat what they have just said, dealing each other a fatal blow.

"No," said Stres. "None of that makes much sense either."

"I agree with you," said his deputy. "But one thing is certain: something must have happened between them for the two women to be in such a state."

"Something happened between them," Stres repeated. "Of course something happened, but what? A terrifying tale from the girl, a terrifying revelation for the mother. Or else . . ."

"There's the house," said the deputy. "Maybe we can find out something."

The great building could be seen in the distance, standing all forlorn on the far side of an open plain. The wet ground was strewn with dead leaves all the way to the house, which had once been one of the grandest and most imposing of the principality, but now had an air of mourning and desertion. Most of the shutters on the upper floors were closed, the eaves were damaged in places, and the grounds before the entrance, with their ancient, drooping, mossy trees, seemed desolate.

Stres recalled the burial of the nine Vranaj brothers three years earlier. There had been one tragedy after another, each more painful than the last, to the point that only by going mad could one erase the memory. But no generation could recall a calamity on this scale: nine coffins for nine young men of a single household in a single week. It had happened five weeks after the grand wedding of the family's only daughter, Doruntine. The principality had been attacked without warning by a Norman army and, unlike in previous campaigns, where each household had had to give up one of their sons, this time all eligible young men were conscripted. So all nine brothers had gone off to war. It had often happened that several brothers of a single household went to fight in far more bloody conflicts, but never had more than half of them fallen in combat. This time, however, there was something very special about the enemy army: it was afflicted with plague, and most of those who took part in the fighting died one way or another, victors and vanquished alike, some in combat, others after the battle. Many a household had two, three, even four deaths to mourn, but only the Vranaj mourned nine. No one could recall a more impressive funeral. All the counts and barons of the principality attended, even the prince himself, and dignitaries of neighbouring principalities came as well.

Stres remembered it all quite clearly, most of all the words on everyone's lips at the time: how the mother, in those days of grief, did not have her only daughter, Doruntine, at her side. But Doruntine alone had not been told about the disaster.

Stres sighed. How quickly those three years had passed! The great double doors, worm-eaten in places, stood ajar. Walking ahead of his deputy, he crossed the courtyard and entered the house, where he could hear the faint sound of voices. Two or three elderly women, apparently neighbours, looked the newcomers up and down.

"Where are they?" Stres asked.

One of the women nodded towards a door. Stres, followed by his deputy, walked into a vast, dimly lit room where his eyes were immediately drawn to two large beds set in opposite corners. Beside each of these stood a woman, staring straight ahead. The icons on the walls and the two great brass candelabra above the fireplace, long unused, cast flickers of light through the atmosphere of gloom. One of the women turned her head towards them. Stres stopped for a moment, then motioned her to approach.

"Which is the mother's bed?" he asked softly.

The woman pointed to one of the beds.

"Leave us alone for a moment," Stres said.

The woman opened her mouth, doubtless to oppose him, but her gaze fell on Stres's uniform and she was silent. She walked over to her companion, who was very old, and both women left without a word.

Walking carefully so as not to make a noise, Stres

approached the bed where the old woman lay, her head in the folds of a white bonnet.

"My Lady," he whispered. "Lady Mother" – for so had she been called since the death of her sons – "it's me, Stres. Do you remember me?"

She opened her eyes. They seemed glazed with grief and terror. He withstood her gaze for a moment and then, leaning a little nearer the white pillow, murmured, "How do you feel, Lady Mother?"

Her expression was unreadable.

"Doruntine came back last night, didn't she?" Stres asked.

The woman looked up from her bed, her eyes saying "yes." Her gaze then settled on Stres as though asking him some question. For a moment, Stres was unsure how to proceed.

"How did it happen?" he asked very softly. "Who brought her back?"

The old woman covered her eyes with one hand, then her head moved in a way that told him she had lost consciousness. Stres took her hand and found her pulse with difficulty. Her heart was still beating.

"Call one of the women," Stres said quietly to his deputy.

His aide soon returned with one of the women who had just left the room. Stres let go of the old woman's hand and walked noiselessly, as before, to the bed where Doruntine lay. He could see her blond hair on the pillow. He felt his heart wrench, but the sensation had nothing to do with what was happening now. An ancient pang that went back to that wedding three years before. On that day, as she rode off on the white bridal steed amidst the throng of relatives and friends, his own heart was suddenly so heavy that he wondered what had come over him. Everyone looked sad, not only Doruntine's mother and brother, but all her relatives, for she was the first girl of the country to marry so far away. But Stres's sorrow was quite unique. As she rode away, he suddenly realised that the feeling he had had for her these last three weeks had been nothing other than love. But it was a love without shape, a love which had never condensed, for he himself had gently prevented it. It was like the morning dew that appears for the first few minutes after sunrise, only to vanish during the other hours of day and night. The only moment when that bluish fog had nearly condensed, had tried to form itself into a cloud, was when she left. But it had been no more than an instant, quickly forgotten.

Stres stood at Doruntine's bed, looking steadily into her face. She was as beautiful as ever, perhaps even more beautiful, with those lips that seemed somehow full and light at the same time.

"Doruntine," he said in a very soft voice.

She opened her eyes. Deep within them he sensed a void that nothing could fill. He tried to smile at her.

"Doruntine," he said again. "Welcome home."

She stared at him.

"How do you feel?" he said slowly, carefully, unconsciously taking her hand. She was burning hot. "Doruntine," he said again, more gently, "you came last night after midnight, didn't you?"

Her eyes answered "yes." He would rather have put

off asking the question that troubled him, but it rose up of itself.

"Who brought you back?"

The young woman's eyes stared steadily back at his own.

"Doruntine," he asked again, "who brought you back?" His voice seemed alien to him. The very question was so fraught with terror that he almost wanted to take it back. But it was too late.

Still she stared at him with those eyes in whose depths he glimpsed a desperate void.

Get it over with now, he told himself.

"You told your mother that it was your brother Kostandin, didn't you?"

Again her look assented. Stres searched her eyes for some sign of madness, but could find no meaning in their utter emptiness.

"I think you must have heard that Kostandin left this world three years ago," he said in the same faint voice. He felt tears well up within him before they suddenly filled her eyes. But hers were tears unlike any others, half-visible, almost impalpable. Her face, bathed by those tears, seemed even more remote. "What's happening to me?" her eyes seemed to say. "Why don't you believe me?"

He turned slowly to his deputy and to the other woman standing near the mother's bed and motioned to them to leave. Then he leaned towards the young woman again and stroked her hand.

"How did you get here, Doruntine? How did you manage that long journey?"

It seemed to him that something strained to fill those unnaturally enlarged eyes.

Stres left an hour later. He looked pale, and without turning his head or speaking a word to anyone, he made his way to the door. His deputy, following behind, was tempted several times to ask whether Doruntine had said anything new, but he didn't dare.

As they passed the church, Stres seemed about to enter the cemetery, but changed his mind at the last minute.

His deputy could feel the glances of curious onlookers as they walked along.

"It's not an easy case," Stres said without looking at his deputy. "I expect there will be quite a lot of talk about it. Just to anticipate any eventuality, I think we would do well to send a report to the prince's chancellery."

To His Highness's Chancellor. Urgent

I believe it useful to bring to your attention events that occurred at dawn on this 11 October in the noble house of Vranaj and which may have unpredictable consequences.

On the morning of 11 October, the aged Lady Vranaj, who, as everyone knows, has been living alone since the death of her nine sons on the battlefield, was found in a state of profound distress, along with her daughter, Doruntine, who, by her own account, had arrived the night before, accompanied by her brother Kostandin, who died three years ago, alongside all his brothers.

Having repaired to the site and tried to speak with the two unfortunate women, I concluded that neither showed any sign of mental instability, though what they now claim, whether directly or indirectly, is completely baffling and incredible. It should be noted at this point that they had given each other this shock, the daughter by telling her mother that she had been brought home by her brother Kostandin, the mother by informing her daughter that Kostandin, with all her brothers, had long since departed this world.

I tried to discuss the matter with Doruntine, and what I managed to glean from her, in her distress, may be summarised more or less as follows:

One night, not long ago (she does not recall the exact date), in the small city in central Europe where she had been living with her husband since her marriage, she was told that an unidentified traveller was asking for her. On going out, she saw the horseman who had just arrived and who seemed to her to be Kostandin, although the dust of the long journey he had just completed made him almost unrecognisable. But when the traveller, still in the saddle, said that he was indeed Kostandin, and that he had come to take her to her mother as he had promised before her marriage, she was reassured. (Here we must recall the stir caused at the time by Doruntine's engagement to a man from a land so far away, the opposition of the other brothers, and

14

especially the mother, who did not want to send her daughter so far off, Kostandin's insistence that the marriage take place, and finally his solemn promise, his besa, that he would bring her back himself whenever their mother yearned for her daughter's company.)

Doruntine told me that her brother's behaviour seemed rather strange, since he did not get off his horse and refused to go into the house. He insisted on taking her away as soon as possible, and when she asked him why she had to leave in such haste – for if the occasion was one of joy, she would don a fine dress, and if it was one of sorrow, she would wear mourning clothes – he said, with no further explanation, "Come as you are." His behaviour was scarcely natural; moreover, it was contrary to all the rules of courtesy. But since she had been consumed with yearning for her family for these three years ("I lived in the most awful solitude," she says), she did not hesitate, wrote a note to her husband, and allowed her brother to lift her up behind him.

She also told me that it had been a long journey, though she was unable to say exactly how long. She says that all she remembers is an endless night, with myriad stars streaming across the sky, but this vision may have been suggested by an endless ride broken by longer or shorter intervals of sleep. It is interesting to note that she does not recall having travelled by day. She may have formed this impression either because she dozed or slept in the saddle all day, so that she no longer remembers the daylight at all, or because she and her escort retired at dawn and went to sleep, awaiting nightfall to continue their journey. Were this to prove correct, it would suggest that the rider wished to travel only by night. In Doruntine's mind, exhausted as she was (not to mention her emotional state), the ten or fifteen nights of the trip (for that is generally how long it takes to travel here from Bohemia) may have blended into a single long – indeed endless – nocturnal ride.

On the way, pressed against the horseman as she was, she noticed quite unmistakably that his hair was not just dusty, but covered with mud that was barely dry, and that his body smelled of sodden earth. Two or three times she questioned him about it. He answered that he had been caught in the rain several times on his way there and that the dust on his body and in his hair, thus moistened, had turned to clots of mud.

When, towards midnight on 11 October, Doruntine and the unknown man (for let us so designate the man the young woman took to be her brother) finally approached the residence of the Lady Mother, he reined in his horse and told his companion to dismount and go to the house, for he had something to do at the church. Without waiting for an answer, he rode towards the church and the cemetery, while she ran to the house and knocked at the door. The old woman asked who was there, and then the few words exchanged *between mother and daughter – the latter having said that it was she and that she had come with Kostandin, the former replying that Kostandin was three years dead – gave to both the shock that felled them.*

This affair, which one is bound to admit is most puzzling, may be explained in one of two ways: either someone, for some reason, deceived Doruntine, posing as her brother with the express purpose of bringing her back, or Doruntine herself, for some unknown reason, has not told the truth and has concealed the manner of her return or the identity of the person who brought her back.

I thought it necessary to make a relatively detailed report about these events because they concern one of the noblest families in the principality and because they are of a kind that might seriously trouble people's minds.

Captain Stres

After initialling his report, Stres sat staring absently at his slanted handwriting. Two or three times he picked up his pen and was tempted to lean over the sheets of paper to amend, recast, or perhaps correct some passage, but each time he was about to put pen to paper his hand froze, and in the end he left his text unaltered.

He got up slowly, put the letter into an envelope, sealed it, and called for a messenger. When the man had gone, Stres stood for a long moment looking out the window, feeling his headache worsen. A crowd of theories jostled one another to enter his head as if through a narrow door. He rubbed his forehead as though to stem the flood. Why would an unknown traveller have done it? And if it was not some impostor, the question was even more delicate: What was Doruntine hiding? He paced back and forth in his office; as he came near the window he could see the messenger's back, shrinking steadily as he threaded his way through the bare poplars. And what if neither of these suppositions was correct, he suddenly said to himself. What if something else had happened, something the mind cannot easily comprehend? Who knows what lies hidden inside us all?

He carried on staring at the windowpane. That rectangle of glass which, at any other time, would have struck him as the most ordinary and innocent thing in the world now suddenly seemed fraught with mystery. It stood in the very midpoint of life, simultaneously separating and connecting the world. "Strange," he mumbled to himself.

Stres managed to snap out of his daydream, turned his back on the window, called his deputy and strode down the stairs.

"Let's go to the church," he said to his deputy when he heard the man's footsteps, then his panting, at his back. "Let's have a look at Kostandin's grave."

"Good idea. When all is said and done, the story only makes sense if someone came back from the grave."

"I wasn't considering anything so ludicrous. I have something else in mind."

His stride lengthened as he said to himself, why am I taking this business so much to heart? After all, there had been no murder, no serious crime, nor indeed any offence of the kind he was expected to investigate in his capacity as regional captain. A few moments ago, as he was drafting his report, this thought had come to him several times: Am I not being too hasty in troubling the prince's chancellery about a matter of no importance? But some inner voice told him he wasn't. That same voice told him that something shocking had occurred, something that went beyond mere murder or any other crime, something that made assassination and similar heinous acts seem mere trifles.

The little church, with its freshly repaired bell tower, was now very near, but Stres suddenly veered off and went straight into the cemetery, not through the iron grille, but through an inconspicuous wooden gate. He hadn't been in the cemetery for a long time, and he had trouble getting his bearings.

"This way," said his deputy as he strode along. "The graves of the Vranaj sons must be over here."

Stres fell in step beside him. The ground was soft in places. Small, soot-blackened icons streaked with candle wax added to the serene and melancholy atmosphere. Some of the graves were covered with moss. Stres stooped to right an overturned cross, but it was heavy and he had to leave it. He walked on. He saw his deputy beckon in the distance: he had found them at last.

Stres walked over. The graves, neatly aligned and covered with slabs of black stone, were identical, made in a shape that suggested a cross as well as a sword, or a man standing with his arms stretched out. At the head of each grave was a small niche for an icon and candles. Beneath it the dead man's name was carved.

"There's his grave," said the deputy, his voice hushed.

Stres looked up and saw that the man had gone pale.

"What's the matter?"

His deputy pointed at the grave.

"Take a good look," he said. "The stones have been moved."

"What?" Stres leaned forward to see what his aide was pointing to. For a long moment he examined the spot carefully, then stood up straight. "Yes, it's true. There's been some disturbance here."

"Just as I told you," said the deputy, his satisfaction in seeing that his chief shared his view mixed with a new surge of fear.

"But that doesn't mean much," Stres remarked.

His deputy turned and looked at him with surprise. His eyes seemed to say, sure, a commander must preserve his dignity in all circumstances, but there comes a time when one must forget about rank, office and such formalities. A battered sun strove to break through the clouds. They looked up, in some astonishment, but neither uttered the words each might have expected to hear in such circumstances.

"No, it doesn't mean anything," Stres said. "For one thing, the slabs could have subsided by themselves, as happens eventually in most graves. Moreover, even if someone did move them, it might well have been an unknown traveller who moved the gravestones before perpetrating his hoax to make it look like the dead man had risen from his grave."

The deputy listened open-mouthed. He was about to

say something, perhaps to raise some objection, but Stres carried on talking.

"In fact, it is more likely that he did it after leaving Doruntine near the house. It's possible he came here then and moved the gravestones before he went off."

Stres, who now seemed weary, let his gaze wander over the field that stretched before him, as if seeking the direction in which the unknown traveller had ridden off. From where they stood they could see the two-storey Vranaj house, part of the village, and the highway, which disappeared into the horizon. It was here on this ground, between the church and that house of sorrow, that the mysterious event of the night of 11 October had occurred. *Go on ahead. I have something to do at the church . . .*

"That's how it must have happened," Stres said. "Unless she's lying."

"'Unless *she* is lying?'" his deputy parroted. "And who, sir, might *she* be?"

Stres didn't answer. The sun at their back, though still a little hazy, now drew their shadows on the ground.

"She . . . Well, Doruntine herself, or else her mother. Or anybody: you, me . . . What's so mysterious about that?" Stres exclaimed.

His deputy shrugged. Little by little the colour had returned to his cheeks.

"I will find that man," Stres said suddenly, raising his voice. The words came harshly through his teeth, with a menacing ring, and his deputy, who had known Stres for years, felt that the passion his chief brought to the search for the unknown man went well beyond the duties of his office. As they walked away, the deputy allowed himself to glance now and again at his boss's shadow. It revealed more of Stres's disquiet than the man himself. It even seemed to him that one of the two halves of Stres's twin characters was standing beside the other, to help him solve the mystery.

CHAPTER TWO

Stres issued an order that reached all the inns and some of the relays along the roads and waterways before the day was out. In it he asked that he be informed if anyone had seen a man and woman riding the same horse or two separate mounts, or travelling together by some other means, before midnight on 11 October. If so, he wanted to be informed which roads they had taken, whether they had stayed at an inn, whether they had ordered a meal for themselves or fodder for their horse or horses, and, if possible, what their relationship seemed to be. Finally, he also wanted to know whether anyone had seen a woman travelling alone.

"They can't escape us now," Stres said to his deputy when the chief courier reported that the circular containing the order had been sent to even the most remote outposts. "A man and a woman riding on the same horse. Now that was a sight you wouldn't forget, would you? For that matter, seeing them on two horses ought to have had more or less the same effect."

"That's right," his deputy said.

Stres stood up and began pacing back and forth between his desk and the window.

"We should certainly find some sign of them, unless they sailed in on a cloud."

His deputy looked up.

"But that's exactly what this whole affair seems to amount to: a journey in the clouds!"

"You still believe that?" Stres asked with a smile.

"That's what everyone believes," his aide replied.

"Other people can believe what they like, but we can't."

A gust of wind suddenly rattled the windows, and a few drops of rain splattered against them.

"Mid-autumn," Stres said thoughtfully. "I have always noticed that the strangest things always seem to happen in autumn."

The room grew silent. Stres propped his forehead with his right hand and stood for a moment watching the drizzling rain. But of course he could not stay like that for long. In the emptiness of his mind, a pressing question emerged and persisted: Who could that unknown horseman have been? Within a few minutes, dozens of possibilities crossed his mind. Clearly, the man was aware, if not of every detail, at least of the depth of the tragedy that had befallen the Vranaj family. He knew of the death of the brothers, and of Kostandin's *besa*. And he knew the way from that central European region to Albania. But why? Stres almost shouted. Why had he done it? Had he hoped for some reward? Stres opened his mouth wide, feeling that the movement would banish his weariness.

The notion that the motive had been some expected reward seemed crude, but not wholly out of the question. Everyone knew that, after the death of her sons, the Lady Mother had sent three letters to her daughter, one after the other, imploring her to come to her. Two of the messengers had turned back, claiming that it had been impossible to carry out their mission: the distance was too great, and the road passed through warring lands. In keeping with their agreement with her, they refunded the old woman half the stipulated fee. The third messenger had simply disappeared. Either he was dead or he had reached Doruntine but she had not believed him. More than two years had passed since then, and the possibility that he had brought her back so long after he set out was more than remote. Perhaps the mysterious traveller meant to extort some reward from Doruntine but had been unable to pass himself off to her as Kostandin. No, Stres thought, the reward theory doesn't stand up. But then why had the unknown man gone to Doruntine in the first place? Was it just a commonplace deception, an attempt to kidnap her and sell her into slavery in some godforsaken land? But that made no sense either, for he had in fact brought her back home. The idea that he had set out with the intention of kidnapping her and had changed his mind en route seemed highly implausible to Stres, who understood the psychology of highwaymen. Unless it was a family feud, some vendetta against her house or her husband's? But that seemed unlikely as well. Doruntine's family had been so cruelly stricken by fate that human violence could add nothing to its distress. Nevertheless, a careful consultation of the noble family's archives – the wills, acts of succession, old court cases – would be wise. Perhaps something could be found that would shed some light on these events. But what if it was only the trick of an adventurer who simply felt like galloping across the plains of Europe with a young woman of twenty-three in the saddle? Stres breathed a deep sigh. His mind's eye wandered back to the vast expanse he had seen on the one occasion he had crossed it, when his horse's hooves, as they pounded through puddles, had shattered the image of the sky, the clouds and the church steeples reflected in them, and the trampling of such things in the mud had struck him as so destructive, so apocalyptic that he had gone as far as to cry out to the Lord for forgiveness. A thousand and one thoughts tumbled through his mind, but he kept returning to the same basic question: Who was the night rider? Doruntine claimed she hadn't seen him clearly at first; she thought he was Kostandin, but he was covered with dust and almost unrecognisable. He had never dismounted, had declined to meet anyone from his brother-in-law's family (though they knew each other, for they had met at the wedding) and had wanted to travel only by night. So he was determined to keep himself hidden. Stres had forgotten to ask Doruntine whether she had ever caught a glimpse of the man's face. It was essential that he ask her that question. In any event, it could not reasonably be doubted that the traveller had been careful to conceal his identity. It was insane to imagine that it could really have been Kostandin, although that was by no means the only issue at stake here. Obviously he wasn't Kostandin, but by this time Stres was even beginning to doubt that the girl was Doruntine.

He pushed the table away violently, stood up and left in haste, striding across the field. The rain had stopped. Here and there the weeping trees were shaking off the last shining drops. Stres walked with his head down. He reached the door of the Vranaj house in less time than he thought possible, strode through the long corridor where he found even more women attending the afflicted mother and daughter, and entered the room where they both languished. From the door he saw Doruntine's pale face and her staring eyes, now with blue-black crescents beneath them. How could he have doubted it? Of course it was her, with that look and those same features that her distant marriage hadn't altered, except perhaps to sprinkle them with the dust of foreignness.

"How do you feel?" he asked softly as he sat down beside her, already regretting the doubts he had harboured.

Doruntine's eyes were riveted on him. There was something unbearable about that ice-cold stare into the abyss, and Stres was the first to look away.

"I'm sorry to have to ask you this question," he said, "but it's very important. Please understand me, Doruntine, it's important for you, for your mother, for all of us. I want to ask you whether you ever saw the face of the man who brought you back."

Doruntine carried on staring at him.

"No," she finally answered, in a tiny voice.

Stres sensed a sudden rift in the delicate relations between them. He had a mad desire to seize her by the shoulders and shout, "Why aren't you telling me the truth?

How could you have travelled for days and nights with a man you believed was your brother without ever looking at his face? Didn't you want to see him again? To kiss him?"

"How can that be?" he asked instead.

"When he said that he was Kostandin and that he had come to get me I was so confused that a terrible dread seized me."

"You thought something bad had happened?"

"Of course. The worst thing. Death."

"First that your mother was dead, then that it was one of your brothers?"

"Yes, each of them in turn, including Kostandin."

"Is that why you asked him why he had mud in his hair and smelled of sodden earth?"

"Yes, of course."

Poor woman, thought Stres. He imagined the horror she must have felt if she thought, even for an instant, that she was riding with a dead man. For it seemed she must have spent a good part of the journey haunted by just that fear.

"There were times," she went on, "when I drove the idea from my mind. I told myself that it really was my brother, and that he was alive. But . . ."

She stopped.

"But . . ." Stres repeated. "What were you going to say?"

"Something stopped me from kissing him," she said, almost inaudibly. "I don't know what."

Stres stared at the curve of her eyelashes, which fell now to the ridge of her cheekbones.

"I wanted so much to take him in my arms, yet I never had the courage, not even once."

"Not even once," Stres repeated.

"I feel such terrible remorse about that, especially now that I know he is no longer of this world."

Her voice was more animated now, her breathing more rapid.

"If only I could make that journey again," she sighed, "if only I could see him just once more!"

She was absolutely convinced that she had travelled in the company of her dead brother. Stres wondered whether he ought to let her believe that or tell her his own suspicions.

"So, you never saw his face," he said. "Not even when you parted and he said, 'Go on ahead, I have something to do at the church'?"

"No, not even then," she said. "It was very dark and I couldn't see a thing. And throughout the journey I was always behind him."

"But didn't you ever stop? Didn't you stop to rest anywhere?"

She shook her head.

"I don't remember."

Stres waited until she was once again looking him straight in the eyes.

"But didn't you wonder if he was hiding something from you?" Stres asked. "He didn't want to set foot on the ground, even when he came to get you; he never so much as turned his head during the whole journey; and judging by what you've told me, he wanted to travel only by night. Wasn't he hiding something?"

"It did occur to me," she replied. "But since he was dead, it was only natural for him to hide his face from me."

"Or maybe it wasn't Kostandin," he said suddenly.

Doruntine looked at him a long while.

"It amounts to the same thing," she said calmly.

"What do you mean, the same thing?"

"If he was not alive, then it's as if it wasn't him."

"That's not what I meant. Did it ever occur to you that this man may not have been your brother, alive or dead, but an impostor, a false Kostandin?"

Doruntine gestured no.

"Never," she said.

"Never?" Stres repeated. "Try to remember."

"I might think so now," she said, "but that night I never had any such doubt, not for a moment."

"But now you might?"

As she stared deeply into his eyes once more, he tried to decide just what the main ingredient in her expression was: grief, terror, doubt, or some painful longing. All these were present, but there was more; there was still room for something more, some unknown feeling, or seemingly unknowable, perhaps because it was a combination of all the others.

"Maybe it wasn't him," Stres said again, moving his head closer to hers and looking into her eyes as though into the depths of a well. A wetness of tears rose up.

Stres tried to fathom an image in them. At times he thought that from deep down something like a ghost – the face of the night rider – would come into focus. But his impatient desire to grasp it was bound up with a no less acute feeling of fear.

"I don't know what to do," she said between sobs.

He let her cry in silence for a while, then took her hand, pressed it gently and, after glancing at her mother in the other bed, where she seemed to be asleep, left noiselessly.

Reports from innkeepers soon began to come in. From long experience Stres was sure that by the end of the week their numbers would double. That would be due not just to greater awareness among innkeepers, but because travellers, knowing they were under surveillance, in spite of themselves, would start behaving in an increasingly suspicious manner.

The reports referred to all manner of comings and goings, from the most mundane, such as those of the *Saturdaners*, the peasants who, unlike others, went to market on Saturdays, to the wobbly gait of the simpleminded, the only ones who could make Stres smile even when he was in a bad mood. Two or three of the reports sounded like descriptions of his own movements on his last trip back home. "On 7 October, in the evening, someone who was hard to make out in the half-light, was riding along on the Count's Road, about a mile from the Franciscan monastery. All that could be seen for sure was that he was holding some heavy burden in his arms, it could have been a person or a cross."

Stres shook his head. On the evening of 7 October, he had indeed crossed the Count's Bridge on horseback, about a mile from the Franciscan monastery. But he hadn't been clutching a living being or a cross. He scratched "No" across the top of each report. No, nowhere had anyone seen a man and woman riding on the same horse or on two horses, nor a woman travelling alone, either on horseback or in a carriage. Although no reports had yet arrived from the most distant inns, Stres was irritated. He had been sure that he would find some trace of them. Is it possible, he wondered, as he read the reports. Could it be that no human eye had spotted them? Was everyone asleep as they rode through the night? No, impossible, he told himself in an effort to boost his own morale. Tomorrow someone would surely come forward and say that he had seen them. If not tomorrow, then the next day. He was sure he would find some seeing eye.

In the meantime, acting on Stres's orders, his deputy was sifting carefully through the family archives, seeking some thread that might lead to the solution to the puzzle. At the end of his first day's work, his eyes swollen from going through a great pile of documents, he reported to his chief that the task was damnable and that he would have preferred to have been sent out on the road, from inn to inn, seeking the trail of the fugitives rather than torturing himself with those archives. The Vranaj were one of the oldest families in Albania and had kept documents for two hundred, and sometimes three hundred, years. These were written in a variety of languages and alphabets, from Latin to Albanian, in characters ranging from Cyrillic to Gothic. There were old deeds, wills, legal judgments, notes on *the chain of blood*, as they called the family tree, that went back as far as the year 881, citations, decorations. The documents included correspondence about marriages. There were dozens of letters, and Stres's deputy set aside the ones dealing with Doruntine's marriage, intending to examine them at his leisure. Some of them had been drafted in Gothic characters, apparently in German, and sent to Bohemia. Others, and these seemed to him even more noteworthy, were copies of letters sent by the Lady Mother to her old friend Count Thopia, lord of the neighbouring principality, from whom, it seemed, she requested advice about various family matters. The Count's answers were in the archives too. In two or three letters over which Stres's aide cast a rapid eye, the Lady Mother had in fact confessed to the Count her reservations about Doruntine's marriage to a husband from so far away, soliciting his view on the matter. In one of them – it must have been among the most recent – she complained about her terrible loneliness, the words barely legible (one felt that it had been written in a shaky hand, at an advanced age). The brides of her sons had departed one by one, taking their children with them and leaving her alone in the world. They had promised to come back to visit her, but none had done so, and in some sense she felt she could hardly blame them. What young woman would want to return to a house that was more ruin than home and on which, it was said, the seal of death had been fixed?

Stres listened attentively to his deputy, although the latter had the impression that his chief's attention sometimes wandered.

"And here," Stres finally asked, "what are they saying here?"

The deputy looked at him, puzzled.

"Here," Stres repeated. "Not in the archives, but here among the people, what are they saying about it?"

His deputy raised his arms helplessly.

"Naturally everyone is talking about it."

Stres let a moment pass before adding, "Yes, of course. That goes without saying. It could hardly be otherwise."

He closed his desk drawer, pulled on his cloak and left, bidding his deputy a good night.

His path home took him past the gates and fences of the single-storey houses that had sprung up since the town, not long ago as small and quiet as the surrounding villages, had become the county seat. The porches on which people whiled away the summer evenings were deserted now, and only a few chairs or hammocks had been left outside in the apparent hope of another mild day or two before the rigours of winter set in.

But though the porches were empty, young girls, sometimes in the company of a boy, could be seen whispering at the gates and along the fences. As Stres approached, they stopped their gossiping and watched him pass with curiosity. The events of the night of 11 October had stirred everyone's imagination, girls and young brides most of all. Stres guessed that each one must now be dreaming that someone – brother or distant friend, man or shadow – would some day cross an entire continent for her.

"So," his wife said to him when he got home, "have you finally found out who she came back with?"

Taking off his cloak, Stres glanced covertly at her, wondering whether there was not perhaps a touch of irony in her words. She was tall and fair, and she looked back at him with the hint of a smile, and in a fleeting instant it occurred to Stres that though he was by no means insensitive to his wife's charms, he could not imagine her riding behind him, clinging to him in the saddle. Doruntine, on the other hand, seemed to have been born to ride like that, hair streaming in the wind, arms wrapped around her horseman.

"No," he said drily.

"You look tired."

"I am. Where are the children?"

"Upstairs playing. Do you want to eat?"

He nodded yes and lowered himself, exhausted, into a chair covered with a shaggy woollen cloth. In the large fireplace tepid flames licked at two big oak logs but were unable to set them ablaze. Stres sat and watched his wife moving back and forth.

"As if all the other cases were not enough, now you have to search for some vagabond," she said through a clinking of dishes.

She made no direct reference to Doruntine, but somehow her hostility came through.

"Nothing I can do about it," said Stres.

The clatter of dishes got louder.

"Anyway," his wife went on, "why is it so important to find out who that awful girl came home with?" This time the reproach was aimed in part at Stres.

"And what makes her so awful?" he said evenly.

"What, you don't think so? A girl who spends three years wallowing in her own happiness without so much as a thought for her poor mother stricken with the most dreadful grief? You don't think she's an ingrate?"

Stres listened, head down.

"Maybe she didn't know about it."

"Oh, she didn't know? And how did she happen to remember so suddenly three years later?"

Stres shrugged. His wife's hostility to Doruntine was nothing new. She had shown it often enough; once they had even fought about it. It was two days after the wedding, and his wife had said, "How come you're sitting there sulking like that? Are all of you so sorry to see her go?" It was the first time she had ever made such a scene.

"She left her poor mother alone in her distress," she went on, "and then suddenly took it into her head to come back just to rob her of the little bit of life she had left. Poor woman! What a fate!"

"It's true," Stres said. "Such a desert—"

"Such hellish solitude, you mean," she broke in. "To see her daughters-in-law leave one after the other, most of them with small children in their arms, her house suddenly dark as a well. But her daughters-in-law, after all, were only on loan, and though they were wrong to abandon their mother-in-law in her time of trouble, who can cast a stone at them when the first to abandon the poor woman was her only daughter?"

Stres sat looking at the brass candelabra, astonishingly similar to the ones he had seen that memorable morning in the room where Doruntine and her mother lay in their sickbeds. He now realised that everyone, each in his own way, would take some stand in this affair, and that each person's attitude would have everything to do with their station in life, their luck in love or marriage, their looks, the measure of good or ill fortune that had been their lot, the events that had marked the course of their life, and their most secret feelings, those that people sometimes hide even from themselves. Yes, that would be the echo awakened in everyone by what had happened, and though they would believe they were passing judgement on someone else's tragedy, in reality, they would simply be giving expression to their own.

In the morning a messenger from the prince's chancellery delivered an envelope to Stres. Inside was a note stating that the prince, having been informed of the events of 11 October, ordered that no effort be spared in bringing the affair to light so as to forestall what Stres himself feared, any uneasiness or misapprehension among the people.

The chancellery asked that Stres notify the prince the moment he felt that the matter had been resolved.

Hmm, Stres said to himself after reading the laconic note a second time. The moment he felt that the matter had been resolved. Easy enough to say. I'd like to see you in my shoes.

He had slept badly, and in the morning he again encountered the inexplicable hostility of his wife, who hadn't forgiven him for failing to endorse her judgement of Doruntine with sufficient ardour, though he had been careful not to contradict her. He had noticed that this sort of friction, though it did not lead to explosions, was in fact more pernicious than an open dispute, which was generally followed by reconciliation.

Stres was still holding the letter from the chancellery when his deputy came in to tell him that the cemetery watchman had something to report.

"The cemetery watchman?" Stres said in astonishment,

eying his aide reproachfully. He was tempted to ask, "You're not still trying to convince me that someone has come back from the grave?" but just then, through the half-open door, he saw what appeared to be the watchman in question.

"Bring him in," Stres said coldly.

The watchman entered, bowing deferentially.

"Well?" said Stres looking up at the man, who stood rigid as a post.

The watchman swallowed.

"I am the watchman at the church cemetery, Mister Stres, and I would like to tell you—"

"That the grave has been violated?" Stres interrupted. "I know all about it."

The watchman was taken aback.

"I, I," he stammered, "I meant—"

"If it's about the gravestone being moved, I know all about it," Stres interrupted again, unable to hide his annoyance. "If you have something else to tell me, I'm listening."

Stres expected the watchman to say, "No, I have nothing to add," and had already leaned over his desk again when, to his great surprise, the man spoke.

"I have something else to tell you."

Stres raised his head and looked sternly at him, making it clear that this was neither the time nor the place for jokes.

"So you have something else to tell me?" he said in a sceptical tone. "Well, let's hear it."

The watchman, still disconcerted by the coolness of his reception, watched Stres lift his hands from the papers spread out on his desk as if to say, "Well, you've taken me away from my work, are you satisfied? Now let's hear your little story."

"We are uneducated people, Mister Stres," the man said timidly. "Maybe I don't know what I'm talking about, please excuse me, but I thought that, well, who knows—"

Suddenly Stres felt sorry for the man and said in a milder tone, "Speak. I'm listening."

What's the matter with me? he wondered. Why do I take out on others the irritation I feel over this business?

"Speak," he said again. "What is it you have to tell me?"

The watchman, somewhat reassured, took a deep breath and began.

"Everyone claims that one of the Lady Mother's sons came back from the grave," he said, staring straight at Stres. "You know more about all that than I do. Some people have even come over to the cemetery to see whether any stones have been moved, but that's another story. What I wanted to say is about something else—"

"Go on," said Stres.

"One Sunday, not last Sunday or the one before, but the one before that, the Lady Mother came to the cemetery, as is her custom, to light candles at the graves of each of her sons."

"Three Sundays ago?" Stres asked.

"Yes, Mister Stres. She lit one candle for each of the other graves, but two for Kostandin's. I was standing very near her at the time, and I heard what she said when she leaned towards the niche in the gravestone."

The watchman paused briefly again, his eyes still fixed on the captain. Three Sundays ago; in other words, Stres thought to himself, not knowing quite why he made the calculation, a little more than two weeks ago.

"I have heard the lamentations of many a mother," the watchman went on, "hers included. But never have I shuddered as I did at the words she spoke that day."

Stres, who had raised his hand to his chin, listened avidly.

"These were not the usual tears and lamentations," the watchman explained. "What she spoke was a curse."

"A curse?"

The watchman took another deep breath, making no attempt to conceal his satisfaction at having finally captured the captain's undivided attention.

"Yes, sir, a curse, and a frightful one."

"Go on," Stres said impatiently. "What kind of curse?"

"It is hard to remember the exact words, I was so shaken, but it went something like this: 'Kostandin, have you forgotten your promise to bring Doruntine back to me whenever I longed for her?' As you probably know, Mister Stres, I mean almost everybody does, Kostandin had given his mother his *besa* to—"

"I know, I know," said Stres. "Go on."

"Well, then she said: 'Now I am left alone in the world, for you have broken your promise. May the earth never receive you!' Those were her words, more or less."

The watchman had been observing Stres's face as he spoke, expecting the captain to be horrified by his terrible tale, but when he'd finished it seemed clear that Stres was thinking of other things. The watchman's self-assurance vanished.

"I thought I ought to come and tell you, in case it was any use," he said. "I hope I haven't disturbed you."

"No, not at all," Stres hastened to answer. "On the contrary, you did well to come. Thank you very much."

The watchman bowed respectfully and left, still wondering whether or not he had made a mistake in coming to tell his story.

Stres still seemed lost in thought. A moment later, he felt another presence in the room. He looked up and saw his deputy, but quickly dismissed him. How could we have been so stupid? he said to himself. Why in the world didn't we talk to the mother? Though he had gone twice to the house, he had questioned only Doruntine. The mother might well have her own version of events. It was an unpardonable oversight not to have spoken to her.

Stres looked up. His deputy stood before him, waiting.

"We have committed an inexcusable blunder," Stres said.

"About the grave? To tell you the truth, I did think of it, but—"

"What are you babbling about?" Stres interrupted. "It has nothing to do with the grave and all these ghost stories. The moment the watchman told me of the old woman's curse, I said to myself, how can we account for our failure to talk to her? How could we have been such idiots?"

"That's a point," said the deputy guiltily. "You're right."

Stres stood up abruptly.

"Let's go," he said. "We must make amends at once."

A moment later they were in the street. His deputy tried to match Stres's long strides.

"It's not only the curse," Stres said. "We have to find out what the mother thinks of the affair. She might be able to shed new light on the mystery."

"You're right," said the deputy, whose words, punctuated by his panting, seemed to float off with the wind and fog. "Something else struck me while I was reading those letters," he went on. "Certain things can be gleaned from them – but I won't be able to explain until later. I'm not quite sure of it yet, and since it's so out of the ordinary—"

"Oh?"

"Yes. Please don't ask me to say more about it just yet. I want to finish going through the correspondence. Then I'll give you my conclusions."

"For the time being, the main thing is to talk to the mother," Stres said.

"Yes, of course."

"Especially in view of the curse the cemetery watchman told us about. I don't think he would have invented that."

"Certainly not. He's an honest, serious man. I know him well."

"Yes, especially because of that curse," Stres repeated. "For if we accept the fact that she uttered that curse, then there is no longer any reason to believe that when Doruntine said, from outside the house, 'Mother, open the door, I've come back with Kostandin' (assuming she really spoke those words), the mother believed what she said. Do you follow me?"

"Yes. Yes I do."

"The trouble is, there's another element here," Stres went on without slowing his pace. "Did the mother rejoice to see that her son had obeyed her and had risen from the grave or was she sorry to have disturbed the dead? Or is it possible that neither of these suppositions is correct, that there was something even darker and more troubling?"

"That's what I think," said the deputy.

"That's what I think too," added Stres. "The fact that the old mother suffered so severe a shock suggests that she had just learned of a terrible tragedy."

"Yes, just so," said the aide. "That tallies with the suspicion I mentioned a moment ago . . ."

"Otherwise there's no explanation for the mother's collapse. Doruntine's is understandable, for now she learns of the death of her nine brothers. The mother's, on the other hand, is harder to understand. Wait a minute, what's going on here?"

Stres stopped short.

"What's going on?" he repeated. "I think I hear shouts—"

They weren't far from the Vranaj residence and they peered at the old house.

"I think I do too," said the aide.

"Oh my God," said Stres, "I hope the old woman's not dead! What a ghastly mistake we've made!"

He set off again, walking faster. He splashed through the puddles and the mud, trampling rotting leaves.

"What madness!" he muttered, "what madness!"

"Maybe it's not her," said the deputy. "It could be Doruntine."

"What?" Stres cried, and his aide realised that the very idea of the young woman's death was unthinkable to his chief.

They covered the remaining distance to the Vranaj house without a word. On both sides of the road tall poplars dismally shook off the last of their leaves. Now they could clearly make out the wailing of women.

"She's dead," said Stres. "No doubt about it."

"Yes, the courtyard is thick with people."

"What's happened?" Stres asked the first person they met.

"At the Vranaj's!" the woman said. "Both are dead, mother and daughter."

"It can't be!"

She shrugged and walked away.

"I can't believe it," Stres muttered again, slowing his pace. His mouth was dry and tasted terribly bitter.

The gates of the house yawned wide. Stres and his deputy found themselves in the courtyard surrounded by a small throng of townspeople milling about aimlessly. Stres asked someone else and got the same answer: both of them were dead. From inside came the wailing of the mourners. Both of them, Stres repeated to himself, stunned.

He felt himself being jostled on all sides. He no longer had the slightest desire to pursue the inquiry further, or even to try to think clearly about it. In truth, the idea that it might be Doruntine who was dead had assailed him several times along the road, but he had rejected it each time. He simply could not believe that both no longer lived. At times, even though the idea horrified him, it was

Doruntine's death that had seemed to him most likely, for in riding with a dead man, which was what she herself believed she had done, she had already moved, to some degree, into the realm of death.

"How did it happen?" he asked no one in particular in that whirlwind of shoulders and voices. "How did they die?"

The answer came from two or three voices at once.

"The daughter died first, then the mother."

"Doruntine died first?"

"Yes, Captain. And for the aged mother, it's plain that there was nothing left but to close the circle of death."

"What a tragedy! What a tragedy!" someone near them said. "All the Vranaj are gone, gone for ever!"

Stres caught sight of his deputy, swept along, like himself, in the crowd. Now the mystery is complete, he thought. Mother and daughter have carried their secret to the grave. He thought of the nine tombs in the churchyard and almost shouted out loud: "You have left me on my own!" They had gone, abandoning him to this horror.

The crowd was in turmoil, diabolically agitated. The captain felt so stressed that he thought his head would burst. He wondered where the greater danger lay – in this swirling crowd or inside himself.

"The Vranaj are no more!" a voice said.

He raised his head to see who had uttered those words, but his eyes, instead of seeking out someone in the small crowd, rose unconsciously to the eaves of the house, as though the voice had come from there. For some moments he did not have the strength to tear his eyes away. Blackened and twisted by storms, jutting out from the walls, the beams of the wide porches expressed better than anything else the dark fate of the lineage that had lived under that roof.

CHAPTER THREE

From the four corners of the principality people flocked to the funeral of the Lady Mother and her daughter. Since time immemorial, events have always been one of two kinds: those that bring people together and those that tear them asunder. The first kind can be experienced and appreciated at market days, crossroads or coaching inns. As for the second, each of us takes them in, or is consumed by them, in solitude. It soon became apparent that the funeral belonged to both categories at once. Although at first sight it seemed to belong to the crowd and the street, what people said about it brought to the surface all that had been whispered or imagined within the walls of every house, and brought confusion to everyone's mind.

Like any disquiet that gestates at first in solitary pain before coming out into the open, rumours about Doruntine grew and swelled up, changing in the most unforeseeable ways. An endless stream of people dragged the story behind them but were yet drawn forward by it. As they sought to give it a shape they found acceptable, they were themselves altered, bruised or crushed by it.

High-born folk with family arms painted on their carriage doors, wandering monks, ruffians and all manner of other people filled and then emptied the high road as they made their way on horseback, in vehicles, but mostly on foot to the county town.

Funeral services had been set for Sunday. The bodies lay in the great reception hall that had been unused since the death of the Vranaj sons. In the gleam of the candles the family's ancient emblems, the arms and icons on the walls, as well as the masks of the dead, seemed covered with a silver dust.

Beside the majestic bronze coffins (Lady Mother had stipulated in her will that a large sum be set aside for her funeral), four professional mourners, seated on carved chairs, led the lamentations. Twenty hours after the deaths, the wailing of the mourners in the reddish gleam of the coffins' reflection had become more regulated, though more solemn. Now and then the mourners broke their keening with lines of verse. One by one, or all four in unison, they recalled various episodes in the saga of this unprecedented tragedy.

In a trembling voice, one of the mourners sang of Doruntine's marriage and of her departure for a distant land. A second, her voice more tremulous still, lamented the nine boys who, so soon after the wedding, had fallen in battle against the plague-ridden army. The third took up the theme and sang of the grief of the mother left alone. The fourth, recalling the mother's visit to the cemetery to put her curse upon the son who had broken his *besa*, sang these words:

A curse be on thee, Kostandin!
Do you recall the solemn promise you made?
Or has your *besa* rotted with you in the grave?

Then the first mourner sang of the resurrection of the son who had been cursed, and of his journey by night to the land where his married sister lived:

If it's joy that brings you here
I'll wear a dress that's fair.
If it's grief that brings you here
Weeds is what I must wear.

While the third responded with the dead man's words:

Come, sister mine, come as you are.

Then the fourth and first mourners, responding one to the other, sang together of the brother's and sister's journey, and of the astonishment of the birds they passed on the way:

Strange things have we seen beyond count
Save a living soul and a dead man
Riding by on the same mount.

The third mourner told of their arrival at the house and of Kostandin's flight towards the graveyard. Then the fourth concluded the lament, singing of Doruntine's knocking at the door, of the words with which she told her mother that her brother had brought her home, so as to keep his promise, and of her mother's response from within the house:

> Kostandin died and was buried as he must.
> Three years have gone since he was laid to rest.
> Why then is he not now just soil and dust?

After a chorus of lamentations by all the women present, the mourners rested briefly, then took up their chants again. The words with which they punctuated their wailing varied from song to song. Some verses were repeated, others changed or were replaced completely. In these new songs, the mourners summarised episodes recounted in the earlier recitals, or else elaborated a passage they had previously mentioned only fleetingly or omitted entirely. Thus it was that one chant gave greater prominence to the background of the incident, or to the great Vranaj family's happier days, or the doubts about Doruntine's marriage to a husband from a distant land, and Kostandin's promise to bring his sister back whenever their mother wished. In another all this was recalled only briefly, and the mourners would linger instead on that dark journey, recounting the words that passed between dead brother and living sister. In yet another song all this was treated more briskly, while new details were offered, such as her brother's quest for Doruntine as he drifted from dance to dance (for a festival was under way in Doruntine's village at that time) and what the horseman said of the girls of the village: "Beautiful all, but their beauty leaves me cold."

The people Stres had sent to keep their ears open took careful note of the tenor of these laments and reported to him at once. The captain sat near the window through which the cold north wind blew and, seeming numb, examined the reports, taking up his pen and underlining individual words or whole lines.

"However much we might rack our brains day and night to find an explanation," he said to his deputy, "the mourners will go on in their own way."

"That's true," his aide replied. "They have no doubt at all that he returned from the dead."

"A legend is being born right before our eyes," Stres said, handing him the sheaf of reports with their underlined passages. "Just look at this. Until two days ago, the songs gave little detail, but since last night, and especially today, they have taken shape as a well-defined fable."

The deputy cast an eye over the pages of underlined verses and words, dotted with brief marginal notes. In places, Stres had drawn question marks and exclamation points.

"Which doesn't mean that we can't get something out of the mourners anyway," he said, with the hint of a smile.

"That's right. I've noticed that an ancient way of bewailing the dead has recently come back into use. It's called 'lamenting within the law'."

"Yes", the deputy concurred.

"I don't know if the phrase exists in any other language, but as a servant of the law, I am, for my own part, struck by such an expression to describe women's wailing at a funeral."

"Indeed", said the deputy.

"Maybe it means that this kind of keening means

more than it appears to mean. That it tends to *become* a law."

His aide was at a loss for a reply.

Through the window you could see the main road, and on it a continuing stream of people coming to attend the burial. Local inns, as well as those for miles around, were overflowing. There were old friends of the family and relatives by marriage. There were representatives of both churches, Byzantium and Rome, as well as members of the prince's family and other lords of neighbouring principalities and counties. Count Thopia, the Lady Mother's old friend, unable to make the journey (whether for reasons of ill health or because of a certain chill that had arisen between him and the prince, no one could say), had sent one of his sons to represent him.

The burial took place on Sunday morning as planned. The road was too narrow to accommodate the crowd, and the long cortège made its way with some difficulty to the church. Many were compelled to cross ditches and cut through the fields. A good number of these people had been guests at Doruntine's wedding not so long ago, and the doleful tolling of the death knell reminded them of that day. The road was the same from the Vranaj house to the church, the same bells tolled, but on this day they sounded very different – protracted and muffled, as if obeying the laws of another kingdom. But apart from that, there was much that was similar: as in the wedding procession three years before, the members of the funeral cortège craned their necks to see the hearse in the same way they had gaped at the bridal steed; the road itself again seemed unable to contain such a milling throng, be it gathered in joy or in grief, and pushed many aside.

Between Doruntine's marriage and her burial, her nine brothers had died. It was like a nightmare of which no more than a confused memory remained. It had lasted two weeks, the chain of calamity seemingly endless, as though death would be satisfied only when it had closed the door of the house of Vranaj for ever. After the first two deaths, which happened on a single day, it seemed as if fate had at last spent its rage against the family, and no one could have imagined what the morrow would bring. No one thought that two more brothers, borne home wounded the evening before, would die just three days later. Their wounds hadn't seemed dangerous, and the members of the household had thought them far less serious than the afflictions of the two who had died. But when they were found dead on that third day, the family, already in mourning, this new grief compounding the old, was struck by an unendurable pain, a kind of remorse at the neglect with which the two wounded brothers had been treated, at the way they had been abandoned (in fact they hadn't been abandoned at all, but such was the feeling now that they were dead). They were mad with sorrow – the aged mother, the surviving brothers, the young widowed brides. They remembered the dead men's wounds, which, in hindsight, seemed huge. They thought of the care they ought to have lavished on them, care which they now felt they had failed to provide, and they were stricken with guilt. The death of the wounded men was doubly painful, for they felt that they had held two lives in their hands and had let them slip away. A few days later, when death visited their household again with an even heavier tread, carrying off the five remaining brothers, the aged mother and the young widows sank into despair. God himself, people said, doesn't strike twice in the same place, but calamity had struck the house of Vranaj as it had done nowhere else. Only then did people hear that the Albanians had been fighting against an army sick with the plague, and that the wounded and most of those who had returned from the war alive would probably suffer the very same fate.

In three months the great house of Vranaj, once so boisterous and full of joy, was transformed into a house of shadows. Only Doruntine, who had left not long before, was unaware of the dreadful slaughter.

The church bell continued to toll the death knell, but among the many who had come to this burial it would have been hard to find a single one who had any distinct memory of the funerals of the nine brothers. It had all happened so nightmarishly, in deep shadow. Coffins were carried out of the Vranaj house nearly every day for more than a week. Many could not recall clearly the order in which the young men had died, and, before long, would be hard pressed to say which of the brothers fell on the battlefield, which died of illness, and which of the combination of his wounds and the terrible disease.

Doruntine's marriage, on the contrary, was an event each and every one remembered in minute detail, one of those that time has a way of embellishing, not necessarily because they are so unforgettable in and of themselves, but because they somehow come to embody everything in the past that was beautiful, or considered so, but is no more. Moreover, it was the first time a young girl of the country had married so far away. This kind of marriage had stirred controversy since time immemorial. Various opinions were expressed, and there were endless conflicts and clashes over it. One group was adamant that local marriages, or at least those within the same village or region, kept the clan free from turmoil and especially from suspect foreign blood. They used as a warning to naysayers the plight of coastal towns like Durrës and Lezhë, where the noble race of the Arberësh had been obliged to mix with all kinds of newcomers. Their prime example was Maria Matrenga, a woman famed for her beauty, who had married a man from another county, and as a result of the distance, the different climate and different customs of her husband's abode, had wilted and finally faded away.

Those who favoured distant marriages made the opposite claim. They invoked the ancient *kanun*, the customary law that prohibited marriage within the four-hundredth degree of relatedness, and scared folk by hinting at the results of inbreeding. To counter the sad story of Maria Matrenga, they reminded people of Palok the Idiot, a seventeen-year-old retard whose parents were close cousins, and who could be seen wandering around the village at all hours.

The two camps fought it out for a long time. At times it seemed that the celestial tale of Maria Matrenga, sprinkled with gold dust like an icon, was in the ascendant, especially at twilight and at the change of seasons; but along came damp and smelly days, when the spittle and stutter of the poor cretin struck fear into people's hearts.

The distant marriage faction had begun to gain ground, but although those who feared inbreeding were easily dissuaded from local marriages, they were equally pained by the prospect of separation. In the beginning, then, the distances were kept small, and marriages two, four, even seven mountains away were countenanced. But then came the striking separation with Doruntine, divided from her family by half a continent.

Now, as the throng following along behind the procession of invited guests headed slowly towards the church, people talked, whispered, recalled the circumstances of Doruntine's marriage, the reluctance of her mother and the brothers who opposed the union, Kostandin's insistence that the marriage take place and his *besa* to his mother that he would always bring Doruntine back to her. As for Doruntine herself, no one knew whether she had freely consented to the marriage. More beautiful than ever, on horseback among her brothers and relatives – who were also mounted – misty with tears, as custom requires of every young bride, she was a wraith already belonging more to the horizon than to them.

All this now came to mind as the procession followed the same path the throng of guests had taken then. And just as crystal shines the more brightly on a cloth of black velvet, so the memory of Doruntine's marriage against the background of grief now gained in brilliance in the minds of all those present. Henceforth it would be difficult for people to think of the one without the other, especially since everyone felt that Doruntine looked as beautiful in her coffin as she had done astride the horse caparisoned for the wedding. Beautiful, but to what end? they murmured. No one had partaken of her beauty. Now the earth alone would enjoy it.

Others, in voices even more muted, spoke of her mysterious return, repeating what people had told them or denying it.

"It seems," someone said, "that Stres is trying to solve the mystery. The prince himself has ordered him to get to the root of it."

"Believe me," a companion interrupted, "there's no mystery about it. She returned to close the circle of death, that's all."

"Yes, but how did she come back?"

"Ah, that we shall never know. It seems that one of her brothers rose from the grave by night to go and fetch her. That's what I heard, it's really astounding. But some people claim that – I know, I know, but don't say it, it's a sin to say such things, especially on the day of her burial. We should rather pray for the poor girl, let the earth not weigh on her too heavily!"

Talk turned once again to the wedding of three years ago, and many felt that the funeral was only its extension, or, more exactly, was the wedding itself, turned upside down. After her bridal journey, Doruntine had simply gone on another outing, one that was macabre . . . with a dead man, or . . . an unidentified . . . Well, whoever it was, it was a most unusual journey . . . or rather, an unnatural one . . . and what's more, with a corpse . . . or worse still, with a . . . But let's drop all that, it's a sin to speak of such things. May God forgive the sinners that we are, and may the earth lie lightly upon her!

And people cut short their discussions, tacitly agreeing that a few days hence, perhaps even on the morrow, once the dead were buried and tranquillity restored, they would speak of this again, perhaps less guardedly, and surely with greater malice.

Which is exactly what happened. Once the burial was over and the whole story seemed at an end, a great clamour arose, the like of which had rarely been heard. It spread in waves through the surrounding countryside and rolled on farther, sweeping to the frontiers of the principality, spilling over its borders and cascading through neighbouring principalities and counties. It was as if many of the people who had attended the burial had carried bits of it away to sow throughout the land.

There were some folk who had prayed for Doruntine on Sunday at the funeral, asking over and over again that the dust and mud treat her kindly and not weigh too heavily on her breast. But now it didn't occur to them that the calumnies they were putting about were more crushing than any amount of earth or stone.

Passing from ear to ear by word of mouth, the rumour was borne by every breath of air and certainly conveyed many a reproach, of the sort that everyone refrains from expressing directly but is prepared, in such circumstances, to evoke in roundabout ways. And as it grew more distant it began to dilate and change its shape like a wandering cloud, though its essence remained immutable: a dead man had come back from the grave to keep the promise he had made to his mother: to bring his married sister back to her from far away whenever she so wished.

Barely a week had gone by since the burial of the two women when Stres was urgently summoned to the Monastery of the Three Crosses. The archbishop of the principality awaited him there, having come expressly on a matter of the greatest importance.

Expressly on a matter of the greatest importance, Stres repeated to himself again and again as he crossed the plain on horseback. What could the archbishop possibly want of him? The prelate did not leave his archiepiscopal seat very often, especially to travel in such awful weather.

A chill wind blew over the frosty, autumnal plain. On either side of the road, as far as the eye could see, despondent hayricks looked as if they were slowly collapsing on themselves. Stres pulled up the collar of his riding cape. What if it had to do with the Doruntine story, he wondered. But he rejected that possibility out of hand. Ridiculous! What did the archbishop have to do with it? He had enough thorny problems of his own, especially since tension in the Albanian territories between the Catholic Church of Rome and the Orthodox Church had reached fever pitch. Some years before, when the spheres of influence of Catholicism and Orthodoxy had become more or less defined, the principality remaining under the sway of the Byzantine Church, Stres had thought that this endless quarrel was at last drawing to a close. Not at all. The two churches had once more taken up their struggle for the allegiance of individual Albanian princes and counts. Information regularly reaching Stres from the inns and relay posts suggested that in recent times Catholic missionaries had intensified their activities in the principalities. Perhaps that was the reason for the archbishop's visit – but then Stres himself was not involved in those matters. It was not he who issued safe conduct passes. No, Stres said to himself, I have nothing to do with that. It must be something else.

He would find out soon enough what it was all about. There was no point in racking his brains now. There was probably a simple explanation: the archbishop may have come for some other reason – a tour of inspection, for instance – and decided incidentally to avail himself of Stres's services in resolving this or that problem. The spread of the practice of magic, for instance, had posed a problem for the church, and that did fall within Stres's remit. Yes, he told himself, that must be it, sensing that he had finally found some solid ground. Nevertheless, it was only a small step from the practice of magic to a dead man rising from his grave. No! – he almost said it aloud – the archbishop can have nothing to do with Doruntine! And spurring his horse, he quickened his pace.

It was really cold. The houses of a hamlet loomed briefly somewhere off to his right, but soon he could see nothing but the plain again, with the haystacks drifting towards the horizon. The puddles beneath his horse's hooves reflected nothing, and thus seemed hostile to him. *The plain is in mourning . . .* he muttered, repeating one of the lines of the professional mourners' chants. He had been astonished to come across the phrase again in his informers' reports. He'd certainly heard it said of a person that he or she was in grief, or in mourning . . . But not of a landscape!

The Monastery of the Three Crosses was still some distance away. Along that stretch of road, Stres kept turning the same ideas over in his mind, but in a different order now. He brought himself up short more than once: nonsense, ridiculous, not possible. But though he resolved repeatedly not to think about it for the rest of the journey, he couldn't stop wondering why the archbishop had summoned him.

It was the first time Stres had ever met the archbishop in person. Without the chasuble in which Stres had seen him standing in the nave of the church in the capital, the archbishop seemed thin, slender, his skin so pale, so diaphanous, that you almost felt you could see what was happening inside that nearly translucent body if you looked hard enough. But Stres lost that impression completely the moment the archbishop started to speak. His voice did not match his physique. On the contrary, it seemed more closely related to the chasuble and mitre which he had set aside, and which he would no doubt have kept by his side if he had not had such a strangely powerful voice.

The archbishop came straight to the point. He told Stres that he had been informed of an alleged resurrection said to have occurred two weeks before in this part of the country. Stres took a deep breath. So that was it after all! The most improbable of all his guesses had been correct. What had happened, the archbishop went on, was evil, more evil and far-reaching than it might seem at first sight. He raised his voice. Only frivolous minds, he said, could take things of this kind lightly. Stres felt himself blush and was about to protest that no one could accuse him of having taken the matter lightly, that on the contrary he had informed the prince's chancellery at once, while doing his utmost to throw light on the mystery. But the archbishop, as if reading his mind, broke in.

"I was informed of all this from the outset and issued express instructions that the whole affair be buried. I must admit that I never expected the story to spread so far."

"It is true that it has spread beyond all reason," said Stres, opening his mouth for the first time.

Since the archbishop himself admitted that he had not foreseen these developments, Stres thought it superfluous to seek to justify his own attitude.

"I undertook this difficult journey," the archbishop went on, "in order to gauge the scope of the repercussions for myself. Unfortunately, I am now convinced that they are catastrophic."

Stres nodded in agreement.

"Nothing less would have induced me to take to the highway in this detestable weather," the prelate continued, his penetrating eyes still fixed on Stres. "Now, do you understand the importance the Holy Church attaches to this incident?"

"Yes, Monsignor," said Stres. "Tell me what I must do."

The archbishop, who apparently hadn't expected this question so early on, sat motionless for a moment, as if choking down an explanation that had suddenly proved unnecessary. Stres sensed he was on edge.

"This affair must be buried," he said evenly. "Or rather, one aspect of it, the one that is at variance with the truth and damaging to the Church. Do you understand me, Captain? We must deny the story of this man's resurrection, reject it, unmask it, prevent its spread at all costs."

"I understand, Monsignor."

"Will it be difficult?"

"Most certainly," said Stres. "I can prevent an impostor

or slanderer from speaking, but how, Monsignor, can I stop such a widespread rumour from spreading further? That is beyond my power."

A cold flame glimmered in the archbishop's eyes.

"I cannot prevent the mourners from singing their laments," Stres went on, "and as for gossip—"

"Find a way to make the mourners stop their songs themselves," the prelate said sharply. "As for rumour, what you must do is change its course."

"And how can I do that?" Stres asked evenly.

They stared at each other for a long moment.

"Captain," the archbishop finally said, "do you yourself believe that the dead man rose from his grave?"

"No, Monsignor."

Stres imagined that the archbishop had given a sigh of relief. How could the man have dreamed that I was naive enough to credit such insanity, he wondered.

"Then you think that someone else must have brought back the young woman in question?"

"Without the slightest doubt, Monsignor."

"Well then, try to prove it," said the archbishop, "and you will find that the mourners will suspend their songs mid-verse and rumour will change of itself."

"I have sought to do just that, Monsignor," Stres said. "I have done my utmost."

"With no result?"

"Very nearly. Of course there are people who do not believe in this resurrection, but they are in a minority. Most are convinced."

"Then you must see to it that this minority becomes the majority."

"I have done all I can, Monsignor."

"You must do even more, Captain. And there is only one way to manage it: you must find the man who brought the young woman back. Find the impostor, the lover, the adventurer, whatever he is. Track him down relentlessly, wherever he may be. Move heaven and earth until you find him. And if you do not find him, then you will have to create him."

"Create him?"

A flash of cold lightning seemed to pass between them.

"In other words," said the archbishop, the first to avert his eyes, "it would be advisable to bear witness to his existence. Many things seem impossible at first that are crowned with success in the end."

The archbishop's voice had lost its ring of confidence.

"I shall do my best, Monsignor," said Stres.

A silence of the most uncomfortable kind settled over the room. The archbishop, head lowered, sat deep in thought. When he next spoke, his voice had changed so completely that Stres looked up sharply, intrigued. His tone, as polite, gentle, and persuasive as the man himself, now matched his physical appearance perfectly.

"Listen, Captain," said the archbishop, "let us speak frankly."

He took a deep breath.

"Yes, let us speak plainly. I think you are aware of the importance attached to these matters at the Centre. Many things may be forgiven in Constantinople, but there is no indulgence whatever for any question touching on the basic principles of the Holy Church. I have seen emperors slaughtered, roped to wild horses, eyes gouged, their tongues cut out, simply because they dared think they could amend this or that tenet of the Church. Perhaps you remember that two years ago, after the heated controversy about the sex of angels, the capital came close to being the arena of a civil war that would have certainly led to wholesale carnage."

Stres did recall some disturbances, but he had never paid much attention to the sort of collective hysteria which erupted periodically in the Empire's capital.

"Today more than ever," the archbishop went on, "when relations between our Church and the Catholic Church have worsened . . . Nowadays your life is at stake in matters like these. Do I make myself clear, Captain?"

"Yes," said Stres uncertainly. "But I would like to know what all this has to do with the incident we were discussing."

"Quite," said the archbishop, his voice growing stronger now, recovering its deep resonance. "Of course."

Stres kept his eyes fixed upon him.

"Here we have an alleged return from the grave," the prelate continued, "and therefore a resurrection. Do you see what that means, Captain?"

"A return from the grave," Stres repeated. "An idiotic rumour."

"It's not that simple," interrupted the archbishop. "It is a ghastly heresy. An arch-heresy."

"Yes," said Stres, "in one sense it is indeed."

"Not in one sense. Absolutely," the archbishop said, nearly shouting. His voice had recovered its initial gravity. His head was now so close that Stres had to make an effort not to take a step backwards.

"Until now Jesus Christ alone has risen from his tomb! Do you follow me, Captain?"

"I understand, Monsignor," Stres said.

"Well then, He returned from the dead to accomplish a great mission. But this dead man of yours, this Kostandin – that is his name, is it not? – by what right does he seek to ape Jesus Christ? What power brought him back from the world beyond, what message does he bring to humanity? Eh?"

Stres, nonplussed, had no idea what to say.

"None whatsoever!" shouted the archbishop. "Absolutely none! That is why the whole thing is nothing but imposture and heresy. A challenge to the Holy Church! And like any such challenge, it must be punished mercilessly."

He was silent for a moment, as if giving Stres time to absorb the flood of words.

"So listen carefully, Captain." His voice had softened again. "If we do not quell this story now, it will spread like wildfire, and then it will be too late. It will be too late, do you understand?"

Stres returned from the Monastery of the Three Crosses in the afternoon. His horse trotted slowly along the highway, and Stres mulled just as slowly over snatches of the long conversation he had just had with the archbishop. Tomorrow I'll have to start all over again, he said to himself. He had, of course, been working on the case without respite, and had even relieved his deputy of his other duties so that he could spend all his time sifting through the Lady Mother's archives. But now that the capital was seriously concerned at the turn of events, he was going to have to go back to square one. He would send a new circular to the inns and relay stations, perhaps promising a reward to anyone who helped find some trace of the impostor. And he would send someone all the way to Bohemia to find out what people there were saying about Doruntine's flight. This latter idea lifted his spirits for a moment. How had he failed to think of it earlier? It was one of the first things he should have done after the events of 11 October. Well, he thought a moment later, it's never too late to do things right.

He glanced up to see how the weather looked. The autumn sky was completely overcast. The bushes on either side of the road quivered in the north wind, and their trembling seemed to deepen the desolation of the plain. This world has only one Jesus Christ, thought Stres, repeating to himself the archbishop's words. The sound of his horse's tread reminded him that it was this very road that Kostandin had taken. The archbishop had spoken of the dead man with contempt. Come to think of it, Kostandin had never shown much respect for Orthodox priests while he lived. Stres himself hadn't known Kostandin, but his deputy's research into the family archives had produced some initial clues to his personality. Judging from the old woman's letters, Kostandin had been, generally speaking, an oppositionist. Attracted by new ideas, he cultivated them with passion, sometimes carrying them to extremes. He had been like this on the question of marriage. He was against local marriages and, impassioned and extremist in his convictions, had been prepared to countenance unions even at the other end of the world.

The Lady Mother's letters suggested that Kostandin believed that distant marriages, hitherto the privilege of kings and princesses, should become common practice for all. The distance between the families of bride and groom was in fact a token of dignity and strength of character, and he persisted in saying that the noble race of Albanians was endowed with all the qualities necessary to bear the trials of separation and the troubles that might arise from them.

Kostandin had ideas of his own not only on marriage but on many other subjects too, ideas that ran counter to common notions and that had caused the old woman more than a little trouble with the authorities. Stres recalled one such instance, which had to do primarily with the Church. Two letters from the local archbishop to the Lady Mother had been found in the family archives in which the prelate drew her attention to the pernicious ideas Kostandin was expressing and to the insulting comments about the Byzantine Church he had occasionally been heard to utter. To judge by the report that Stres had read, Kostandin and some of his equally pigheaded friends had been against the severance with Rome and the compact with the Eastern Church. And there were other, more important matters, his aide had told him, but these would figure in the detailed report he would submit once he had concluded his investigation.

Stres had not been particularly impressed by this aspect of Kostandin's personality, possibly because he himself harboured no special respect for religion, an attitude that was in fact not uncommon among the officials of the principality. And for good reason: the struggle between

Catholicism and Orthodoxy since time immemorial had greatly weakened religion in the Albanian principalities. The region lay just on the border between the two religions and, for various reasons, essentially political and economic, the principalities leaned now towards one, now towards the other. Half of them were now Catholic, but that state of affairs was by no means permanent, and each of the two churches hoped to win spheres of influence from the other. Stres was convinced that the prince himself cared little for religious matters. He had allies among the Catholic princes and enemies among the Orthodox. In truth, the principality had once been Catholic, turning Orthodox only half a century before, and the Roman Church had not given up hope of bringing it back to the fold.

Stres was a servant of the state, and strived to remain neutral on the issue of religion, which was not really close to his heart in any case. All the same, he wasn't pleased to see a part of Arbëria absorbed by the Eastern Church after a thousand years of Roman Christianity. Indeed, he might well have sought some excuse not to respond to the archbishop's summons were it not for the fact that the prince, eager to avoid poisoning relations with Byzantium, had recently issued an important circular urging all officials of the principality to treat the Church with respect. The circular emphasised that this attitude was dictated by the higher interests of the state and that, consequently, any action at variance with the spirit of the directive would be punished.

All this passed through Stres's mind in snatches as his glance embraced the bleak expanse of the plain. The

October cold filled the air. Suddenly Stres shivered. Behind a bush several paces off the road he caught sight of the skeleton of a horse standing out in all its whiteness. It was a section of the ribcage and the backbone; the skull was missing. My God, Stres thought to himself a little further on, what if that had been *his* horse?

He drew his cloak tighter around him, trying to drive the image from his mind. He felt sad, but it was not a painful sadness. The shape of his melancholy had been softened in the great stretch of plain, in which winter's approach could be read. What possessed you to come out of the earth, what message did you mean to bring us? Stres was astonished at the question, which had risen like a sigh from the depths of his being. He shook his head as if to clear his mind. He who had laughed so derisively at everyone who had believed that story! He smiled bitterly. What nonsense! he said to himself, spurring his horse. What a gloomy afternoon! he thought a moment later. Dusk was falling as he urged his mount into a canter. All the rest of the way to the village he strove to purge his mind of anything connected with the case. He arrived in the dark of night. The lights of the houses shone feebly here and there. From time to time the barking of dogs in the distance broke the night silence. Stres guided his horse not homeward, but towards the town's main street. He had no idea why. Soon he reached the vacant lot that stretched before the house of the Lady Mother. There was no other house to be seen. The dark and dismal mass of the great abandoned building loomed at the far end of a desolate field studded with tall trees that now, in the dark, seemed to droop even more sharply than usual. Stres approached the doorway, gazed for a moment at the darker rectangles of the windows, then turned his horse in the direction from which he had come. He found himself among the trees. A man standing where he now stood could be seen from the door.

The night of 11 October must have been more or less like this one: no moon, but not too dark. It must have been here that Doruntine parted from the unknown horseman. It suddenly occurred to Stres that he had been in this spot before. But his memory of the occasion was all in a muddle, buried under rubble, as it were. For a moment even his horse's hooves went silent. It was as if he was riding through the air. Rubbish, he thought. His imagination was so disturbed that fragments of the incident were sticking to him like flakes of wet snow. The sound of his horse's hooves came back to life and soothed him . . . So this must be where Doruntine parted from the night rider. When her mother opened the door, he was probably riding off, but perhaps she had already seen something from the window. Something that caused that fatal shock . . . Stres turned his horse again. What discovery had the old woman made in the semi-darkness? That the man riding off was her dead son? ("It was my brother Kostandin who brought me back," Doruntine had told her.) Or perhaps, on the contrary, that it was not her son and that her daughter had deceived her? Maybe, but that wouldn't explain her shock. Or perhaps, just before they separated, Doruntine and the unknown rider had embraced one last time in the dark— Enough! Stres said to himself sharply, and turned his horse back towards the road. At the very last moment, with the furtive movement of a man trying to catch a glimpse of someone spying on him in the darkness, he turned his head towards the closed door once more. But there was nothing, only the dark night that seemed to be mocking him.

CHAPTER FOUR

The day after his return from the Monastery of the Three Crosses Stres set to work again to unravel the enigma of Doruntine's return. He drafted a new more detailed directive, ordering the arrest of all suspects, offering in addition a reward to anyone who helped capture the impostor directly or by providing information leading to his arrest. He also instructed his deputy to make a list of all those who had been out of town between the end of September and 11 October, and to look discreetly into the activities of every person on the list. In the meantime, he ordered one of his men to set out at once for the far reaches of Bohemia, in order to investigate locally the circumstances of Doruntine's departure.

The man hadn't yet left when a second directive, even more compelling than the first, came from the prince's chancellery, demanding that the entire matter be brought to light as soon as possible. Stres understood at once that the archbishop must have been in touch with the prince and that the latter, aware of his captain's reluctance to obey Church injunctions, had decided that a fresh personal intervention was required. The directive emphasised that the tense political situation of recent times, in particular relations with Byzantium, required caution and understanding on the part of all officials of the prince.

Meanwhile, the archbishop remained inside the Monastery of the Three Crosses. Why on earth had he holed up there and not moved on? Stres wondered. The old fox had obviously decided to keep an eye on things.

Stres felt more and more nervous. His aide was coming to the end of all that research in the archives. His eyes bleary from the long sessions of reading, he went around looking dreamy.

"You seem sunk in deep meditation," Stres observed jokingly, at a break in his own hectic schedule. "Who knows what you're going to pull out of those archives for us?"

Instead of smiling, the deputy looked strangely at Stres, as if to say you may think it's a laughing matter, but it will take your breath away.

Sometimes, walking to the window as if to rest his eyes on a view of the wide plain, Stres wondered if the truth about Doruntine's tale might not be completely different from what they all assumed, if that macabre ride with an unknown horseman was in fact no more than the product of the girl's sick mind. After all, no one had seen that horseman, and Doruntine's old mother, who had opened the door for her and who was the only witness, had made no such assertion. Good God, he said to himself, could it be that the whole thing never happened? Perhaps Doruntine had somehow learned of the disaster that had befallen her family and, driven mad by the shock, had set out for home on her own. In a state of such deep distress she might have taken much time indeed – months, even years – to complete a journey she believed had taken a single night. That might well explain the flocks of stars she thought she saw streaming across the sky. Besides, someone who believed that the ten-day-and-night journey from Bohemia (for that was the least it could take) had lasted but a single night might well feel that a hundred nights were one. And of course a person in such a state might fall prey to all sorts of hallucinations.

In vain, Stres sought to recall Doruntine's face as it had looked when he saw her for the last time, so that he might detect some sign of mental illness. But her image eluded him. In the end he resolved to drive the theory of madness from his mind, for he feared it might dampen his zeal for the investigation. It will all be cleared up soon enough, he told himself. As soon as my man comes back from Bohemia.

Thirty-six hours after the man's departure, Stres was informed that some relatives of Doruntine's husband had just arrived. At first it was rumoured that her husband himself had come, but it soon became clear that the visitors were his two first cousins.

After dispatching a second messenger to overtake the first and tell him to turn back, Stres hurried to meet the new arrivals, who had taken lodgings at the inn at the crossroads.

The two young men were so alike in bearing and appearance that they might have been taken for twins, though they were not. They were still tired from their long journey and had not yet had time to wash or change their clothes when Stres arrived. He couldn't help staring at their dust-covered hair, and looked at them in so odd a fashion that one, with just the hint of a guilty smile, passed his fingers through his hair and spoke a few words in an incomprehensible tongue.

"What language do they speak?" Stres asked his deputy, who had arrived at the inn shortly before him.

"God knows," was the reply. "It sounds to me like German laced with Spanish. I sent someone to the Old Monastery to fetch one of the monks who speaks foreign languages. He shouldn't be long."

"I have a hard time making myself understood with the little Latin I know," said the innkeeper. "And they massacre it too."

"Perhaps they need to wash and rest a bit," Stres said to the innkeeper. "Tell them to go upstairs if they like, until the interpreter gets here."

The innkeeper passed on Stres's message in his fractured Latin. The visitors nodded agreement and, one behind the other, began climbing the wooden stairs, which creaked as if it might collapse. Stres could not help staring at their dusty cloaks as he watched them go up.

"Did they say anything?" he asked when the staircase had stopped creaking. "Do they know that Doruntine is dead?"

"They learned of her death and her mother's while on their way here," the deputy answered, "and surely other things as well."

Stres began pacing back and forth in the large hall, which also served as the reception room. The others – his aide, the innkeeper and a third man – watched him come and go without daring to break the silence.

The monk from the Old Monastery arrived half an hour later. The two foreigners came down the wooden stairs, whose creaking seemed more and more sinister to Stres's ear. Their hair, now free of most of the journey's dust, was very blond.

Stres turned to the monk and said, "Tell them that I am Captain Stres, responsible for keeping order in this district. I believe they have come to find out what happened to Doruntine, have they not?"

The monk translated these words for the strangers, but they looked blankly at one another, seeming not to understand.

"What language are you speaking?" Stres asked the monk.

"I'll try another," he said without answering the question.

He spoke to them again. The two strangers leaned forward with the pained expressions of men straining to understand what is being said to them. One of them spoke a few words, and this time it was the monk whose face took on a troubled expression. These exchanges of words and grimaces continued for some time until finally the monk spoke several long sentences to which the strangers now listened with nods of great satisfaction.

"Finally found it," said the monk. "They speak a German dialect mixed with Slavonic. I think we'll be able to understand one another."

Stres spoke immediately.

"You have come just in time," he said. "I believe you

have heard what happened to your cousin's wife. We are all dismayed."

The strangers' faces darkened.

"When you arrived I had already sent someone to your country to find out the circumstances of her leaving there," Stres went on. "I hope that we may be able to learn something from you, as you may learn something from us. I believe that all of us have an equal interest in finding out the truth."

The two strangers nodded in agreement.

"When we left," said one of them, "we knew nothing, save that our cousin's wife had gone off suddenly, under rather strange circumstances, with her brother Kostandin."

He stopped and waited for the monk, who kept his pale eyes fixed upon him, to translate his words.

"While en route," the stranger continued, "still far from your country, we learned that our cousin's wife had indeed arrived at her parents' home, but that her brother Kostandin, with whom she said she had left, had departed this life three years ago."

"Yes," said Stres, "that's correct."

"On the way we also learned of the old woman's death, news that grieved us deeply."

The stranger lowered his eyes. A silence followed, during which Stres motioned to the innkeeper and two or three onlookers to keep their distance.

"You wouldn't have a room where we could talk, would you?" Stres asked the owner.

"Yes, of course, Captain. There is a quiet place just over there. Come."

They filed into a small room. Stres invited them to sit on carved wooden chairs.

"We had but one goal when we set out," one of the two strangers continued, "and that was to satisfy ourselves about her flight. In other words, first of all to make sure that she had really reached her own family, and secondly to learn the reason for her flight, to find out whether or not she meant to come back, among other things that go without saying in incidents of this kind."

As the monk translated, the stranger stared at Stres as if trying to guess whether the captain grasped the full meaning of his words.

"For an escapade of this kind, as I'm sure you must realise, arouses . . ."

"Of course," said Stres. "I quite understand."

"Now, however," the visitor continued, "another matter has arisen: this question of the dead brother. Our cousin, Doruntine's husband, knows nothing of this, and you may well imagine that this development gives rise to yet another mystery. If Doruntine's brother has been dead for three years, then who was the man who brought her here?"

"Precisely," Stres replied. "I have been asking myself that question for several days now, and many others have asked it too."

He opened his mouth to continue, but suddenly lost his train of thought. In his mind, he knew not why, he saw in a flash the white bones of the horse lying on the plain that afternoon, as if they had tumbled there from some troubled dream.

"Did anyone see the horseman?" he asked.

"Where? What horseman?" the two strangers said, almost in one voice.

"The one believed to have been her brother, the man who brought Doruntine here."

"Oh, I see. Yes, there were women who happened to be close by. They said they saw a horseman near our cousin's house, and that Doruntine hurried to mount behind him. And then there's also the note she left."

"That's right," Stres said. "She told me about a note. Have you read it?"

"We brought it with us," said the second stranger, the one who had spoken least.

"What? You have the note with you?"

Stres could scarcely believe his ears, but the stranger was already rummaging through his leather satchel, from which he finally took out a letter. Stres leaned forward to examine it.

"It's her handwriting, all right," said the deputy, peering over Stres's shoulder. "I recognise it."

Stres stared with wide eyes at the crude letters, which seemed to have been formed by a clumsy hand. The text, in a foreign language, was incomprehensible. One word, the last, had been crossed out.

"What does it say?" asked Stres, leaning even closer. Only one word was recognisable, her brother's name, spelled differently than in Albanian: *Cöstanthin.* "What do these other words mean?" Stres asked.

"I am going away with my brother Kostandin," the monk translated.

"And the word that's scratched out?"

"It means 'if'."

"So: 'I am going away with my brother Kostandin. And if . . .'" Stres repeated. "What was the 'if' for, and why did she cross it out?"

Was she trying to hide something? Stres thought suddenly. Looking for a way to camouflage the truth? Or was this a final attempt to reveal something? But then why did she suddenly change her mind?

"It could be that she found it hard to explain in this language," said the monk, without taking his eyes from the paper. "The other words, too, are full of mistakes."

All were silent.

Stres's thoughts were focused on one point: he finally had a genuine piece of evidence. From all the fog-shrouded anguish there had at last come a piece of paper bearing words written in her own hand. And the horseman had been seen by those women, so he too was real.

"What day did this happen?" he asked. "Do you remember?"

"It was 29 September," one of them answered.

Now the chronology in turn was coming out of that blanket of fog. One very long night, Doruntine had said, with flocks of stars streaming across the sky. But in fact it was a journey of twelve or, to be exact, thirteen days.

Stres felt troubled. The concrete, incontrovertible evidence with which he had just been provided – Doruntine's note, the horseman who had taken her up behind him, the thirteen-day journey – far from giving him any sense that he was finally making some progress and stood on solid ground, left him with no more than a feeling of great emptiness. It seemed that coming closer to the unreal, far from diminishing it, made it even more terrifying. Stres was not sure quite what to say.

"Would you like to go to the cemetery?" he finally asked.

"Yes, of course," chorused the strangers.

They all went together on foot. From the windows and verandas of the houses, dozens of pairs of eyes followed their path to the church. The cemetery watchman had already opened the gate. Stres went through first, clods of mud sticking to the heels of his boots. The strangers looked absently at the rows of tombstones.

"This is where her brothers lie," said Stres, stopping before a row of black slabs. And here are the graves of the Lady Mother and Doruntine," he continued, pointing to two small mounds of earth into which temporary wooden crosses had been sunk.

The newcomers stood motionless for a moment with their heads bowed. Their hair now resembled the melted candle wax on either side of the icons.

"And that grave over there is Kostandin's."

Stres's voice seemed far away. The gravestone, canted slightly to the right, hadn't been straightened. Stres's deputy searched his chief's face, but understood from his expression that he was not to mention that the gravestone had been moved. The cemetery watchman, who had accompanied the small group and now stood a little to one side, also held his tongue.

"And there you are," Stres said when they had returned to the road. "A row of graves is all that remains of the whole family."

"Yes, it is very sad indeed," said one of the strangers.

"All of us here were most disturbed by Doruntine's return," Stres went on. "Perhaps even more than you were in your land over her departure."

As they walked they spoke again of the young woman's mysterious journey. Whatever the circumstances, there could be no justification for such a flight.

"Did she seem unhappy in your country?" Stres asked. "I mean, surely she must have missed her family."

"Naturally," one of them answered.

"And at first, I suppose, the fact that she did not know your language must surely have increased her sense of solitude. Was she worried about her family?"

"Very much so, especially in recent times."

In such terrible solitude . . .

"Especially in recent times?" Stres repeated.

"In recent times, yes. Since none of her relatives had come to visit her, she was in a state of constant anxiety."

"A state of anxiety?" Stres said. "Then surely she must have asked to come herself?"

"Oh yes, on several occasions. My cousin had told her, 'If no one from your family comes to see you by spring, I will take you there myself.'"

"Indeed?"

"Yes. And in truth she was not alone in her anxiety, for we had all begun to fear that something might have happened here."

"Apparently she didn't want to wait until spring," Stres said.

"It would seem so."

"When he learned of her flight, her husband must surely—"

The two strangers looked at one other.

"Of course. It was all very strange. Her brother had come to fetch her, but how was it he had made no appearance at the house, not even for a moment? Admittedly there had been an incident between Kostandin and our cousin, but so much time had passed since then—"

"An incident? What sort of incident?" Stres interrupted.

"The day of the wedding," his deputy answered, lowering his voice. "The old woman speaks of it in her letters."

"But notwithstanding this incident," the stranger continued, "her brother's behaviour – if indeed it really was her brother – was not justifiable."

"Forgive me," Stres said, "but I wanted to ask you whether her husband thought, even for an instant, that it might not be her brother?"

They looked at each other again.

"Well – how shall I put it? Naturally he suspected it. And needless to say, if it was not her brother, then it was someone else. Anything can happen in this world. But no one would ever have anticipated such a thing. They'd been getting along very well. Her circumstances, it must be admitted, were far from easy, being a foreigner as she was, not knowing the language, and especially worrying so much about her family. But they were fond of each other in spite of everything."

"All the same, to run away like that so suddenly," Stres interrupted.

"Yes, it is strange, we must admit. And it was just in

order to clarify things that, at our cousin's request, we set out on this long journey. But here we have found an even more complicated situation."

"A complicated situation," Stres said. "In one sense that is true enough, but it doesn't alter the fact that Doruntine actually returned to her own people."

He spoke these words softly, like a man who finds it difficult to express himself, and in his own heart he wondered, why on earth are you still defending her?

"That is true," one of the strangers answered. "And in one sense, seen in that light, we find it reassuring. Doruntine indeed came back to her people. But here we have a new mystery: the brother with whom she is said to have made the journey is long since dead. One may therefore wonder who it was that brought her back, for surely someone must have accompanied her here, is that not so? And several women saw the horseman. Why, then, did she lie?"

Stres lowered his head thoughtfully. The puddles in the road were strewn with rotting leaves. He thought it superfluous to tell them that he had already asked himself all these questions. And it seemed equally futile to tell them of his conjecture about an impostor. Now more than ever he doubted its validity.

"I simply don't know what to tell you," he said, shrugging his shoulders. He felt weary.

"Nor do we know what to say," commented one of them, the one who had spoken least so far. "It is all very sad. We are leaving tomorrow. There is nothing more for us to do here."

Stres did not answer him.

It's true, he thought, his mind numb. There is nothing more for them to do here.

The strangers left the next day. Stres felt as though he had only been awaiting their departure to make a cool-headed attempt, perhaps the last, to clear up the Doruntine affair. It was quite evident that the two cousins had come to find out whether Doruntine had told the truth in her note, since her husband had at first suspected infidelity. And perhaps he had been right. Perhaps the story was far more simple than it appeared, as is often true of certain events which, however simple in themselves, seem to have the power to sow confusion in people's minds, as if to prevent discovery of their very simplicity. Stres sensed that he was finally unravelling the mystery. Up to now he had always assumed that there was an impostor in the case. But the reality was otherwise. No one had deceived Doruntine. On the contrary, it was she who had deceived her husband, her mother, and finally everyone else. She tricked us all, Stres thought with a mixture of exasperation and sorrow.

The suspicion that Doruntine had been lying had sprung up in his mind from time to time, only to vanish immediately in the mist that surrounded the whole affair. And that was understandable enough, for there were so many unknowns in the case. Stres had only to recall his initial doubts that the horseman and the night ride were real, or his suspicion that Doruntine had actually left her husband's home months, even years, before. Yes, he had only to remember his theory that she had been suffering from mental illness and all his elegant reasoning seemed merely specious. But the visit of the Bohemian strangers had dispelled all these doubts. Now there was a note, which he had seen with his own eyes, and in it she made mention of her flight with someone. Several women had seen the horseman. And most important of all, a date had been established: 29 September. Now you're stuck, Stres said to himself, not without regret. His satisfaction at the prospect of an early resolution of the mystery was rather muted. Perhaps he had become sentimentally attached to the mystery, and would rather not have seen it brought to light. He even felt himself to have been somehow betrayed.

The whole thing, then, notwithstanding the macabre background, had been no more than a commonplace romance. That was the heart of it. All the rest was secondary. His wife had been right to see it that way from the start. Women sometimes have a special flair for this sort of thing. Yes, that must be it, Stres repeated to himself, as if trying to convince himself as thoroughly as possible. A journey with her lover, though love and sex may well have been blended with grief. But that was just the thing that gave the whole story its special flavour. What wouldn't I give, she had said, to make that journey once more. Yes, of course, Stres said to himself, of course.

He thought of her without resentment, but felt somehow weary. Tentatively at first, then ever more doggedly, his mind began churning in the usual way, trying to reconstruct what might have happened. He thought of the two strangers, now on their way to the heart of Europe and certainly thinking things over just as he was. They must be speaking much more openly between themselves than they did here. They must be mulling over the clues they had turned up themselves or had heard reported by others, the suggestions that this foreign woman, this Doruntine, had had a tendency to deceive her husband.

Little by little Stres filled in the blanks. Some time after her wedding Doruntine comes to realise that she no longer loves her husband. She sulks, regrets having married him. Her distress is compounded by her ignorance of the language, her solitude and her yearning for her family. She recalls the long deliberations over this marriage, the hesitation, the arguments for and against, and all this only deepens her sorrow. To make matters worse, none of her brothers comes to see her. Not even Kostandin, despite his promise. Sometimes she worries, fearing that some misfortune has befallen her family, but she spurns these bleak notions, telling herself that she has the good fortune to have not just one or two brothers but nine, all in the prime of life. She believes it more likely that they have simply forgotten her. They have sent their only sister away, dispatched her beyond the horizon, and now they no longer spare her a thought. Her sadness is paired with mounting hostility towards her husband. She blames him for everything. From the end of the world he had come to fetch her, to ruin her life. Her constant sadness, her lack of joy, becomes tied in her mind with the idea of seeking revenge upon her husband. She resolves to leave him, to go away. But where? She is a young woman of twenty-three, all alone, completely alone, in the middle of a foreign continent. In these circumstances, quite naturally, her only consolation would be some romantic attachment. In an effort to fill the void in her life she initiates one, perhaps not even realising what she is doing. She gives herself to the first man who courts her. It may have been with any passing traveller (for are not all her hopes bound up with the highway?). Without further thought she decides to go away with him. At first she thinks to run off without a word to anyone, but then, at the last minute, moved by a final twinge of remorse for her husband, or perhaps by mere courtesy (for she was raised in a family that held such rules dear), she decides to leave him a note. Here again she may have hesitated. Should she tell him the truth or not? Probably out of simple human respect, in an effort not to injure his self-esteem, she decides to tell him that she is going away with her brother Kostandin. Which is particularly plausible since Kostandin had given his *besa* that he would fetch her on occasions of celebration or grief, and everyone, including her husband, was aware of Kostandin's promise.

So, with no other thought in her head, she rides off with her lover. It matters little whether or not they planned to marry. Maybe she meant to return to her family with him some time later, to explain the situation to her mother and her brothers, to share with them her torment, her solitude (it was so lonely), and perhaps, after hearing her explanation, they might forgive her this adventure and she could live among them with her second husband, never to go away again, ever.

But she thinks all this vaguely. Thrilled by her present joy, she is not inclined to worry too much about the future. She has time, and later she will see. Meanwhile she roams from inn to inn with her lover (they must have sold her jewellery), drunk with happiness.

But this happiness does not last long. In one of these inns (the things one learns in those inns with their great fireplaces during the long autumn nights!) she hears of the tragedy that has befallen her family. Perhaps she learns the full truth, perhaps only a part, or perhaps she simply imagines what must have happened, for she has heard talk of the foreign army sick with the plague that has ravaged half of Albania. She is near to madness. Remorse, horror and anguish drive her to the brink of insanity. She begs her lover to take her home right away, and he agrees. So it is she, Doruntine, who leads the unknown horseman, finding her way with difficulty from country to country, from one principality to the next.

The closer they get to the Albanian border, the more she thinks about what she will say when she is asked, "Who brought you back?" Until now she has given the matter little thought. If only she can get home, she will think of something then. But now the family hearth is no longer far off. She will have to account for her arrival. If she says that she was accompanied by an unknown traveller, she has little chance of being believed. To say openly that she came with her lover is also impossible. Earlier she had thought of these things incoherently, bringing little logic to bear, for the issue seemed of scant importance under the burden of her grief. But now it becomes ever more pressing. As her mind goes in every direction looking for a solution, she suddenly recalls Kostandin's *besa* and makes her decision: she will say that Kostandin kept his word and brought her home. Which means that she knows that he will not be there, that he is absent, therefore she knows that he is dead. She is not yet aware of the scope of the disaster that has struck her family, but she has learned of his death. Apparently she has asked after him in particular. Why? It is only natural for him to occupy a larger place in her mind than the others, since it was he who had promised to come and fetch her. Through the long days of sorrow in her husband's home she had been waiting for him to appear on the dusty road.

And now the house is near. She is so agitated that she has no time to invent a new lie even if she wanted to. She will say that the dead man brought her back. And so she finally knocks at the door. She tells her lover to stay off to one side, to be careful not to be seen; perhaps she arranges to meet him somewhere several days hence. From within the house her mother asks the expected question: With whom have you come? And she answers: With Kostandin. Her mother tells her that he is dead, but Doruntine already knows it. Her lover insists on one last kiss before the door opens, and takes her in his arms in the half-darkness. That is the kiss the old woman glimpses through the window. She is horrified. Does she believe that her son has risen from the grave to bring her daughter back to her? It is a better bet that she assumes that it is not her son, but someone unknown to her. However that may be, whether she thought that Doruntine was kissing a dead man or a living one, the horror she feels is equal. But there's a good chance that the mother thought she saw her kissing a stranger. Her daughter's lie seems all the more macabre: though in mourning, she takes her pleasure with unknown travellers like a common slut.

No one will ever know what happened between mother and daughter, what explanations, curses or tears were exchanged once the door swung open.

Events then move rapidly. Doruntine learns the full

dimensions of the tragedy and, needless to say, loses all contact with her lover. Then the dénouement. Stres's mistake was to have asked, in his very first circular to the inns and relay stations, for information about two riders (a man and woman riding the same horse or two horses) coming into the principality. He should have asked that equal effort be concentrated on a search for any solitary traveller heading for the border. But he had corrected the lapse in his second circular, and he now hoped that the unknown man might still be apprehended, for he must have remained in hiding for some time waiting to see how things would turn out. Even if it proved impossible to capture him here, there was every chance that some trace of his passage would be found, and the neighbouring principalities and dukedoms, strongly subject to Byzantium's influence, could be alerted to place him under arrest the moment he set foot in their territory.

Before going home for lunch, Stres again asked his aide whether he had heard anything from the inns. He shook his head. Stres threw his cloak over his shoulders and was about to leave when his deputy added:

"I have completed my search through the archives. Tomorrow, if you have time, I will be able to present my report."

"Really? And how do things look?"

His deputy stared at him.

"I have an idea of my own," he replied evenly, "quite different from all current theories."

"Really?" Stres said again, smiling without looking at the man. "Goodbye, then. Tomorrow I'll hear your report."

As he walked home his mind was nearly blank. He

thought several times of the two strangers now riding back to Bohemia, going over the affair in their own minds again and again, no doubt thinking what he, in his own way, had imagined before them.

"You know what?" he said to his wife the moment he came in, "I think you were right. There's a very strong chance that this whole Doruntine business was no more than an ordinary romantic adventure after all."

"Oh really?" Beneath her flashing eyes, her cheeks glowed with satisfaction.

"Since the visit of the husband's two cousins it's all becoming clear," he added, slipping off his cloak.

As he sat down by the fire, he had the feeling that something in the house had come to life again, an animation sensed more than seen or heard. His wife's customary movements as she prepared lunch were more lively, the rattling of the dishes more brisk, and even the aroma of the food seemed more pleasant. As she set the table he noticed in her eyes a glimmer of gratitude that quickly dispelled the sustained chill that had marked all their recent days. During lunch the look in her eyes grew still softer and more meaningful, and after the meal, when he told the children to go take their naps, Stres, stirred by a desire he had felt but rarely in these last days, went to their bedroom and waited for her. She came in a moment later, the same gleam in her eyes, her hair, just brushed, hanging loose upon her shoulders. Stres thought suddenly that in days to come, the dead woman would come back often, bringing them physical warmth, as now, or else an icy chill.

He made love to his wife with heightened sensuality.

She too was, so to speak, at fever pitch. She offered herself to him by pushing her pelvis as high as it would go, and he entered her as deeply as he could, as if he were seeking out a second passageway inside her. He managed to get close to it, he felt, to a place where a different kind of damp darkness began, then the lips of the inner vagina drew him in further and invited him to an apparently inaccessible realm. An inhuman *aah* escaped him as his seed managed to spill, or so it seemed, into that other place, the dark kingdom where he would never go. Good God, he mumbled involuntarily as the tension subsided and he could feel himself collapsing all at once.

A few minutes later, lying beside his wife, whose blushing cheeks were lit by a smile, he heard her whisper words which, despite their long intimacy through many years of marriage, she had never dared say to him before. She confessed she had rarely had such strong pleasure and that his organ had never before been so . . . hard . . .

In other circumstances her lack of modesty would have taken him aback, but not today.

"It seems to me," he said without looking at his wife, "that you've got something else to say."

She smiled.

"Well, yes," she replied, "it's a curious sensation . . . I was thinking that it wasn't just very hard . . . but also, how can I put it . . . very cold."

Now it was his turn to smile. He explained that it was a feeling a woman has when she herself is at fever pitch.

As their breathing slowed they lay silent, gazing alternately at the carved wooden ceiling and through the half-shuttered window at the low late autumn sky.

"Look," she said, "a stork. I thought they'd gone long ago."

"A few sometimes stay behind. Laggards."

He could not have said why, but he felt that the conversation about Doruntine, suspended since lunch, now threatened to return. Caressing a lock of hair on her temple, he turned his wife's eyes from the sky, convinced that he had managed, in this way, to escape any further talk of the dead woman.

The next day, before summoning his deputy to get his report on the Vranaj archives, Stres glanced at the files on crimes committed in the last seven days. One burglary. Two murders. One rape.

He ran through the report on the murders. Both of them honour killings. Presumably taking advantage of all the commotion about Doruntine, the killers had seized an opportunity to *take back the blood* in accordance with the ancient *kanun*. Even so, you won't get away with it, Stres muttered. When he reached the sentence, "The marksmen have been arrested," Stres crossed out "marksmen" and replaced it with "murderers". Then he added in the margin: "Put them in chains like ordinary criminals".

"You thought you would get treated as special one more time", he grunted. After lying dormant for many years, the *kanun* seemed for some reason to have come back to life and to be rising from its own ashes. Despite repeated and unambiguous warnings from the prince, who was adamant that only the laws of the state and not those of the *kanun* now held sway, family killings had gone on increasing in number.

Stres underlined "ordinary criminals" before reading the last file. Maria Kondi, aged twenty-seven. Married. Died suddenly as she left mass on Sunday. Raped at night two days after her burial. No bodily harm. Jewellery and wedding ring not stolen.

He rubbed his forehead. It was the second case of necrophilia in recent years. Good God, he sighed, in a sudden fit of weariness. But it wasn't a true rape, just ordinary sex. Almost normal . . .

His deputy looked just as worried as he had the previous day. He also looked very unwell, Stres thought.

"As I have said before, and as I repeated to you yesterday," he began, "my research in these archives has led me to a conclusion about this disturbing incident quite different from those commonly held."

I never imagined that lengthy contact with archives could make a man's face look so much like cardboard, Stres thought.

"And," the deputy went on, "the explanation I have come to is also very different from what you yourself think."

Stres raised his eyebrows in astonishment.

"I'm listening," he said as his aide seemed to hesitate.

"This is not a figment of my imagination," the deputy went on. "It is a truth that became clear to me once I had scrupulously examined the Vranaj archives, especially the correspondence between the old woman and Count Thopia."

He opened the folder he was holding and took out a packet of large sheets of paper yellowed by time.

"And just what do these letters amount to?" Stres asked impatiently.

His deputy took a deep breath.

"From time to time the old woman told her friend her troubles, or asked his advice about family affairs. She had the habit of making copies of her own letters."

"I see," said Stres. "But please, try to keep it short."

"Yes," replied his deputy, "I'll try."

He took another breath, scratched his forehead.

"In some letters, one in particular, written long ago, the old woman alludes to an unnatural feeling on the part of her son Kostandin for his sister, Doruntine."

"Really?" said Stres. "What sort of unnatural feeling? Can you be more specific?"

"This letter gives no details, but bearing in mind other things mentioned in later letters, particularly Count Thopia's reply, it is clear that it was an incestuous feeling."

"Well, well."

Thick drops of sweat stood out on the deputy's forehead. He continued, pretending not to notice his chief's ironic tone.

"In fact, the count immediately understood what she meant, and in his reply," said the aide, slipping a sheet of paper across the table to Stres, "he tells her not to worry, for these were temporary things, common at their ages. He even mentions two or three similar examples in families of his acquaintance, emphasising that it happens particularly in families in which there is only one daughter, as was the case with Doruntine. 'However, alertness and great caution are needed to make this somewhat unnatural emotion revert to normal. In any event, we'll talk about this at length when we see each other again'."

The deputy looked up to see what impression the

reading had had on his chief, but Stres was staring at the tabletop, drumming his fingers nervously.

"Their subsequent letters make no further mention of the matter," the aide went on. "It seems that, as the count predicted, the brother's unhealthy feeling for his sister had become a thing of the past. But in another letter, written several years later, when Doruntine was of marriageable age, the old woman tells the count that Kostandin is unable to conceal his jealousy of any prospective fiancé. On his account, she says, we have had to reject several excellent matches."

"And what about Doruntine?" Stres interrupted.

"Not a word about her attitude."

"And then what?"

"Later, when the old woman told the count of the distant marriage that had just been arranged, she wrote that she herself, alongside Doruntine and most of her sons, had long hesitated, concerned that the distance was too great, but that this time it was Kostandin who argued vigorously for the prospective marriage. In his letter of congratulations, the count told the old woman, among other things, that Kostandin's attitude towards the marriage was not at all surprising, that, on the contrary, in view of what she had told him it was understandable that Kostandin, irritated by the possibility of any local marriage which would have forced him to see his sister united with a man he knew, could more easily resign himself to her marriage to an unknown suitor, preferably a foreigner as far out of his sight as possible. It is a very good thing, the count wrote, that this marriage has been agreed upon, if only for that reason."

The deputy leafed through his folder for a few moments. Stres was staring hard at the floor.

"Finally," the aide continued, "we have here the letter in which the old woman described the wedding to her correspondent, and, among other things, the incident that took place there."

"Ah yes, the incident," said Stres, as if torn from his somnolence.

"Though this incident passed largely unnoticed, or in any event was considered natural enough in the circumstances, it was only because people were unaware of those other elements I have just told you about. The Lady Mother, on the other hand, who was well acquainted with these elements, offers the proper explanation of the event. Having told the count that, after the church ceremony, Kostandin paced back and forth like a madman, and that when they had accompanied the groom's kinsmen as far as the highway, he accosted his sister's husband, saying to him: 'She is still mine, do you understand, mine!' the old woman tells her friend that this, thank God, was the last disgrace she would have to bear in the course of this long story."

Stres's subordinate, apparently fatigued by his long explanation, paused and swallowed.

"That's what these letters come to," he said. "In the last two or three, written after her bereavement, the old woman complains of her loneliness and bitterly regrets having married her daughter to a man so far away. There's nothing else. That's it."

The man fell silent. For a moment the only sound came from Stres's fingers tapping on the table.

"And what does all this have to do with our case?"
His deputy looked up.

"There is an obvious, even direct, connection."

Stres looked at him with a questioning air.

"I think you will agree that there is no denying Kostandin's incestuous feelings."

"It's not surprising," Stres said. "These things happen."

"You will also admit, I imagine, that his stubborn desire to have his sister marry so far away is evidence of his struggle to overcome that perverse impulse. In other words, he wanted his sister to have a husband as far from his sight as possible, so as to remove any possibility of incest."

"That seems clear enough," said Stres. "Go on."

"The incident at the wedding marks the last torment he was to suffer in his own lifetime."

"In his lifetime?" Stres asked.

"Yes," said the deputy, raising his voice for no apparent reason. "I am convinced that Kostandin's unslaked incestuous desire was so strong that death itself could not still it."

"Hmm," Stres said.

"Incest unrealised survived death," his aide went on. "Kostandin believed that his sister's distant marriage would enable him to escape his yearning, but, as we shall see, neither distance nor even death itself could deliver him from it."

"Go on," Stres said drily.

His aide hesitated for a moment. His eyes, burning with an inner flame, stared at his chief, as if to make sure that he had leave to continue.

"Go on," said Stres a second time.

But his deputy was still staring, still hesitating.

"Are you trying to suggest that his unsated incestuous desire for his sister lifted the dead man from his grave?" asked Stres, his voice icy.

"Precisely!" his aide cried out. "That macabre escapade was their honeymoon."

"Enough!" Stres bellowed. "You're talking nonsense!"

"I suspected, of course, that you would not share my view, but that is no reason to insult me, sir."

"You're out of your mind," Stres said. "Completely out of your mind."

"No, sir, I am not out of my mind. You are my superior. You have the right to punish me, to dismiss me, even to arrest me, but not to insult me. I, I—"

"You, you, you what?"

"I have my own view of this matter, and I believe it to be no more than a case of incest, for Kostandin's actions can be explained in no other way. As for the theory, which I have lately heard expressed, that he insisted that his sister marry into a distant family because he had some inkling of the calamity that was soon to befall the family and did not wish to see her so cruelly hurt, I consider it absurd. It is true that Kostandin harboured dark forebodings, but it was the threat of incest that tormented him, and if he sent his sister away, it was to remove her from this danger rather than to ensure that she would escape a calamity of some other kind . . ."

The deputy spoke rapidly, not even pausing for breath, apparently afraid that he would be prevented from speaking all his mind.

"But as I said, neither distance nor death itself allowed him to escape incest. Thus it was that one stifling night he rose from his grave to do what he had dreamed of doing all his life – let me speak, please, do not interrupt – he rose from the earth on that wet and sultry October night and, mounting his gravestone become a horse, set out to live his life's dream. And thus did that sinister honeymoon journey come about, the girl riding from inn to inn, just as you said, not with a living lover but with a dead one. And it was just that heinous fact that her aged mother discovered before she opened the door. Yes, she saw Doruntine kiss someone in the shadows, not the lover or impostor you believed, but her dead brother. What the old woman had feared all her life had finally happened. That was the disaster she discovered, and that was what brought her to her grave—"

"Madman," said Stres, more softly this time, as though murmuring the word to himself. "I forbid you to continue," he said with composure.

His aide opened his mouth, but Stres leapt to his feet and, leaning close to the man's face, shouted, "Not another word, do you hear? Or I'll have you thrown in jail, on the spot, right now. Do you understand?"

"I have spoken my mind," the man replied, breathing with difficulty. "Now I shall obey."

"It's you who are sick," Stres said. "You're the one who's sick, poor man."

He looked for a long moment at his deputy's face, wan from insomnia, and suddenly felt keenly sorry for him.

"I was wrong to assign you to all that research in the

family archives. So many long hours of reading, for someone unused to books—"

The man's feverish eyes remained fixed on his chief.

"You may go now," said Stres in a kindlier voice. "Get some rest. You need rest, do you hear? I am prepared to forget all this nonsense, provided you forget it too, do you follow me? You may go."

His aide rose and left. Stres, smiling stiffly, watched the man's unsteady gait.

I must find that adventurer right away, he said to himself. The archbishop was right, the whole business should have been nipped in the bud to avoid the dangerous consequences it will surely have.

He began to pace the room. He would tighten precautions at every crossing point, assign all his men to the task, suspend all other activity to mobilise them for this one case. He would set everything in motion, he would spare no effort until the mystery was cleared up. I must find the truth, he told himself, as soon as possible. Or else we'll all go mad.

Despite the efforts of Stres's men, acting in concert with Church officiants who lectured the faithful day after day, those who believed that Doruntine had returned with her lover were many fewer than those inclined to think that the dead man had brought her back.

Stres himself examined the list of people who had been out of the district between the end of September and 11 October. The idea that Doruntine might have been brought back by one of Kostandin's friends so that his promise might be fulfilled came to him from time to time, but each time it struck him as hardly credible. Even after the complete list of absentees had been submitted to him and he found, as he had hoped, that the names of four of the dead man's closest friends were on it, he could not bring himself to accept the conjecture. After all, hadn't he himself been away on duty during just that time? On the night he got back his cloak had been so filthy that his wife had asked, Stres, just *where* have you been? Doubt is the mind's first action, and just as he had suspected others, so others had the right to suspect him. And in any event, Kostandin's friends had little trouble proving that all four had been at the Great Games held annually in Albania's northernmost principality. Two of them had even taken part and had won prizes.

In the meantime, it would soon be forty days since the death of mother and daughter. The day would be celebrated according to custom, and the mourners would certainly sing their distressing ballads, without changing a damned word. Stres was well acquainted with the obtuse stubbornness of those little old women. On the seventh day after the deaths, also celebrated according to custom, they had changed nothing despite the warning he had sent them, and they had done the same on the four Sundays that followed. The old crows will caw for another few days, the priest had said, but in the end they'll be quiet. Stres was not too sure about that.

One day he saw them making their way in single file to the abandoned house to take up their mourning, as was the custom. Stres stood, tall and still, at the roadside, dressed in his black cape with the white antler on its collar signifying his rank as an officer of the prince, and he watched the women pass by, dressed all in black, with their cheeks already wetted by the tears they had yet to shed, paying him no attention at all. Stres surmised that they had recognised him, nonetheless, for he thought he could detect in their eyes a glint of irony directed at him, the destroyer of legends. He nearly burst out laughing at the thought that he was engaged in a duel with these mourners, but to his astonishment the thought suddenly turned into a shiver.

In the meantime, the archbishop, to everyone's surprise, had remained at the Monastery of the Three Crosses, though Stres was no longer annoyed about it. Absorbed in his pursuit of the wandering adventurer, he paid little attention to anything else. He had received no clear information from the innkeepers. There had been three or four arrests on the basis of their reports, but all the suspects had been released for lack of evidence. Information was awaited from neighbouring principalities and dukedoms, especially in the northern districts through which the road to Bohemia passed. At times, Stres entertained new doubts and built new theories, only to set them aside at once.

The first snow fell towards the middle of November. Unlike the snow that falls in October, it did not melt, but blanketed the countryside in white. One afternoon, as he was on his way home, Stres, almost unconsciously, turned his horse into the street leading to the church. He dismounted at the cemetery gate and went in, trampling the immaculate snow. The graveyard was deserted, the crosses against the blanket of snow looked even blacker. A few birds, equally dark, circled near the far side of the cemetery. Stres walked until he thought he had found the group of Vranaj graves. He leaned forward, deciphered the inscription on one of the stones, and saw that he had made no mistake. There were no footprints anywhere around. The icons seemed frozen. What am I doing here, he asked himself with a sigh. He felt the peace of the graveyard sweep over him, and the feeling brought with it a strange mental clarity. Dazzled by the glare of the snow, he found himself unable to look away, as if he feared that the clarity might desert him. All at once Doruntine's story seemed as simple as could be, pellucid. Here was a stretch of snow-covered earth in which was buried a group of people who had loved one another intensely and had promised never to part. The long separation, the great distance, the terrible yearning, the unbearable solitude (*It was so lonely* . . .) had tried them sorely. They had strained to reach one another, to come together in life and in death in a state partaking of death and life alike, dominated now by the one, now by the other. They had tried to flout the laws that bind the living together and prevent them from passing back from death to life; they had thereby tried to violate the laws of death, to attain the inaccessible, to gather together once more. For a moment, they thought they had managed it, as in a dream when you encounter a dead person you have loved but realise that it is only an illusion (*I could not kiss him, something held me back*). Then, in the darkness and chaos, they parted anew, the living making her way to the house, the dead returning to his grave (*You go ahead, I have something to do at the church*), and though nothing of the kind had really happened, and quite apart from the fact that Stres could not bring himself to believe that a dead man had risen from his grave, in some sense that was exactly what had happened. The horseman–brother had appeared at a bend in the road and said to his sister, "Come with me." It did not really matter whether it was all in her mind or in the minds of other people. At bottom, it was something that could happen to anyone, anywhere, at any time. For who has never dreamed of someone coming back from far away to spend another moment with them, to sit astride the same horse for a while? Who in the world has not yearned for a loved one, has never said, If only he or she could come back just once, just one more time, to be kissed – but somehow, something stops you from giving that kiss? Despite the fact that it can never happen, never ever. Surely this is the saddest thing about our mortal world, and its sadness will go on shrouding human life like a blanket of fog until its final extinction.

That's what it was all about, Stres said to himself again. All the rest – surmises, inquiries, arguments – was just a pack of mean little lies signifying nothing. He would have liked to linger a while longer on that high ground where his thought flowed so freely, but he could feel the pull of the ordinary world dragging him forever downwards, faster and faster, making him tumble down from on high as soon as it could. He hurried away before he could hit bottom. Looking as drained as a sleepwalker, he stumbled towards his horse, vaulted into the saddle and galloped away, as stiff as ice.

CHAPTER FIVE

It was a wet afternoon, drenched in a fine, steady rain, one of those afternoons when one feels that nothing could possibly happen. Stres, dressed and dozing in an armchair (what else could he do on such a day?), felt his wife's hand gently touch his shoulder.

"Stres, there are people here to see you."

He woke with a start.

"What is it? Was I sleeping?"

"They're asking for you," his wife said. "It's your deputy, and another man with him."

"Oh? Tell them I'll be right down."

His aide and someone Stres didn't know, their hair dripping, stood waiting on the porch.

"Captain," said his deputy the moment he saw his chief, "the man who brought Doruntine back has been captured."

Stres was taken aback.

"How can that be?" he asked.

His deputy was astonished at the surprise evident in

the face of his chief, who showed no sign of satisfaction, as if he hadn't spent weeks trying to find the man.

"Yes, they've caught him at last," he said, still not sure whether his chief had fully grasped what he was talking about.

Stres went on staring at them quizzically. In fact he had understood perfectly. What he wasn't sure of was whether or not the news pleased him.

"But how?" he asked. "How could it happen so suddenly?"

"So suddenly?" his deputy said.

"What I mean is, it seemed so unlikely . . ."

What in the world am I talking about? he said to himself. He had become aware of his own confusion.

It seemed obvious now that the suspicion that had occasionally occurred to him from the deepest recesses of his mind – the suspicion that his wish to track down the supposed lover was in competition with an even fiercer desire never to lay hands on the man at all – was proving to be justified.

"Upon my soul," he mumbled, by way of a reaction, like a man who looks up at the sky to ready himself for growling, "What filthy weather", then asked, "But how did they catch him? And where?"

"They're bringing him in now," answered his deputy. "He'll be here before nightfall. This man is the messenger who brought the news, as well as a report."

The stranger reached into the lining of his leather tunic and took out an envelope.

"He was captured in the next county, in a place called the Inn of the Two Roberts," the deputy said.

"Oh?"

"Here is the re . . . re . . . report," said the stranger, who had a stammer.

Stres took it from him brusquely. Little by little the vague feeling of sadness and regret at the resolution of the mystery gave way to a first surge of cold and dangerous light-headedness. He unsealed the envelope, took out the report, turned it towards the light and began to read the lines written in a handwriting that looked like a pile of angrily scattered pins:

> We hereby dispatch to you this report on the capture of the adventurer suspected of having deceived and brought back Doruntine Vranaj. The information in this report has been taken from that which has been handed over to our authorities, along with the adventurer in question, by the authorities of the neighbouring county, who captured him in their territory, in accordance with our request.
>
> The vagabond was arrested on 14 November in the highway establishment known as the Inn of the Two Roberts. He had been brought there unconscious the night before by two peasants who found him lying in the road in high fever. His appearance and, in particular, his delirious raving immediately aroused the suspicions of the innkeeper and the customers. The snatches of sentences he spoke amounted more or less to this: "There is no need to hurry so. What will we say to your mother? Hold on tight, I can't go any faster, it's dark, you know, I can't see anything. That's what you'll say if anyone

asks you who brought you back. Don't be afraid,
none of your brothers is still alive."

The innkeeper alerted the local authorities,
who, after hearing his testimony and that of the
customers, decided to arrest the vagabond and, in
accordance with our request, to hand him over to
us at once. In keeping with the instructions that I
have received from the capital, I will send him on
to you immediately, but I thought it useful also to
send you this information by a swift messenger as
well, so that you might be fully informed about the
matter in case you wish to interrogate the prisoner
at once.

I send you my greetings.
Captain Gjikondi, of the border region.

Stres looked up from the sheet he was holding and glanced
quickly at his deputy, then at the messenger. So it was just
as he had imagined: she had run off with a lover.

His recent dreaminess was instantly supplanted by a
wave of anger among the most violent he had ever experienced. It was like a blast of wind that choked his breathing,
clouded his mind, and probably affected his speech as
well. Like a stinging nettle, it allowed no exemptions. Now
they'll find out who Stres really is! They'll soon see what
happens when you try to take him for a ride! He would
show them, scoundrels all, and this time the gloves
would be off! He was going to make a clean sweep of all
that filth and shit! What he was about to do would make
those crooks and parasites lose their taste for wasting his

time for a hundred years – and he'd do the same to those slimy mourners, those snakes in the grass who'd been boiled in their own venom! He'd put an end to their evil propaganda! To think that he, fearless Stres, had yielded to those crazy hags! Such lies they told, O Lord, such abominations . . .

Troubled by his own irritation, and realising he had gone too far, Stress suddenly retreated into silence.

"When are they due to arrive?" he asked the messenger after a long pause.

"In two hours, three at most."

It was only then that Stres noticed that the messenger's boots were caked with mud to the knees. He took a deep breath. The ideas that had come to him in the graveyard snow three days before seemed very far away.

"Wait for me," he said, "while I get my cape."

He went back inside and, donning his long riding cape, told his wife, "The man who brought Doruntine back has been captured."

"Really?" she said. She could not see his face, for a flap of his cape, like the wing of a great black bird, had come between them and kept their eyes from meeting.

Stres kept his mouth shut all the way, but despite that, as he watched the captain's stride, especially the way his boots dealt with the puddles, his companion grasped that the police chief was still just as angry and that his indignation could be read in the movement of his legs just as accurately, if not more so, as from his speech.

They had been waiting more than two hours for the carriage that was to bring the prisoner. The floorboards creaked plaintively under Stres's boots as he paced back and forth, as was his custom, between his work table and the window. His deputy dared not break the silence; and the messenger, whose wet clothes gave off a musty odour, sat slumped in a wooden chair, and snored.

Stres could not help stopping at the window from time to time. As he gazed out at the plain and waited for the carriage to appear, he felt his mind turn slowly numb. The same steady and monotonous rain had been falling since morning, and anyone's arrival, from whatever quarter, seemed quite inconceivable under its dreary regularity.

He touched the thick paper of the report with his fingers as if to convince himself that the man he was waiting for was really coming. We can't go any faster, it's dark, you see. He repeated to himself the delirious prisoner's words. Don't be afraid, none of your brothers is still alive . . .

He's the one, Stres said to himself. Now he was sure of it. Just as he had imagined. He recalled the moment in the cemetery, that day in the snow when he told himself that it was all lies. Well, it wasn't all lies, he now thought, his eyes fixed on the chilly expanse. The plain stretched to infinity in the grey rain, and the snow itself had melted or withdrawn into the distance without a trace, as if to help him forget everything that that great day had pumped into the captain's head.

The dusk was getting thicker. On either side of the road an occasional idler could be seen, no doubt awaiting the arrival of the carriage. News of the arrest had apparently spread.

The messenger, dozing in his corner, made a sound like a groan. The deputy seemed lost in thought. Stres had heard no further mention of that incest theory of his. He must be embarrassed now.

The messenger let out another groan and half opened his eyes. They had a demented look.

"What's going on?" he asked. "Are they here yet?"

No one answered. Stres went to the window for perhaps the hundredth time. The plain was now so gloomy that it was hard to make out anything. But soon the arrival of the carriage was heralded, first by a far-off rumbling, and then by the clatter of its wheels.

"Good Lord! At last," said Stres's deputy, shaking the messenger by the shoulder.

Stres ran down the stairs, followed by his aide and the messenger. The carriage was rolling up as they got to the threshold. A few people were following along in the dark. Others could be heard running from farther off. The carriage came to a halt and a man dressed in the uniform of an officer of the prince got off.

"Where is Captain Stres?" he asked.

"I am he," said Stres.

"I believe you have been informed that—"

"Yes," Stres interrupted. "I know all about it."

The man in uniform seemed about to add something, but then turned and headed for the carriage, leaned in through the window and said a few words to the people inside.

"Light a lantern," someone called out.

The curtain over the carriage window was drawn back, revealing a forest of legs that jiggled about in such a way that you could not tell whether the people attached to them were embracing each other or having a fight.

Stres knew from experience that the way the legs of a criminal or his escort moved told you everything about the rest of the man, and so he understood that the prisoner had been restrained in the severest fashion, with his hands tied behind his back.

"It's him! It's him!" whispered the people who had gathered around.

The flickering gleam of the lantern revealed no more than half the face of the man in irons, a face bizarrely streaked with mud. The men who had brought him handed him over to two of Stres's men, who took hold of him, as the first ones had, by the armpits. The shackled man offered no resistance.

"To the dungeon," Stres said shortly. "What about you, what do you mean to do now?" he added, addressing the man in uniform, who seemed to be the commander of the small detachment.

"We're going back at once," he replied.

Stres stood there until the carriage shook into motion, then turned towards the building. At the very last moment he paused on the threshold. He sensed the presence of people in the half-darkness. In the distance he heard the footsteps of a man running towards them.

"What are you all waiting for, good people?" Stres asked quietly. "Why don't you go home and go to bed? We have to stay up, it's part of our job, but why should you stand around here?"

No answer came from the shadows. The light of the

lantern flickered briefly as if terrified by those waxy twisted faces, then abandoned them to the darkness.

"Good night," said Stres, entering the building and, lantern in hand, following his deputy down the staircase that led to the dungeon. The smell of mould choked him. He felt suddenly uneasy.

His aide pushed open the iron door of the dungeon and stood aside to let his chief pass. The prisoner was slumped on a pile of straw. Sensing a presence, he looked up. Stres could just make out his features in the gleam of the lantern. He seemed handsome, even marked as he was by the mud and the blows he had suffered. Stres's eyes were drawn involuntarily to the man's lips, and those human lips – cracked in the corners by fever, yet strangely alien to those shackles, those guards, those orders – suggested to Stres more than any other detail that he had before him the man who had made love to Doruntine.

"Who are you?" asked Stres icily.

The prisoner looked up. His expression, like his lips, seemed foreign to the setting. Seducer's eyes, Stres said to himself.

"I am a traveller, officer," the man answered. "An itinerant seller of icons. They arrested me. Why, I don't know. I am very sick. I shall lodge a complaint."

He spoke a laboured but correct Albanian. If he really was a seller of icons, he had apparently learned the language for his trade.

"Why did they arrest you?"

"Because of some woman I don't even know, whom I've never seen. Someone called Doruntine. They told me

I made a long journey on horseback, with her behind me, and all sorts of other rubbish."

"Did you really travel with a woman? More precisely, did you bring a woman here from far away?" Stres asked.

"No, sir, I did not. I have travelled with no woman at all, at least not in several years."

"About a month ago," said Stres.

"No. Absolutely not!"

"Think about it," said Stres.

"I don't have to think about it," said the shackled man in a booming voice. "I am sorry to see, sir, that you too apparently subscribe to this crazy idea. I am an honest man. I was arrested while lying on the roadside in agony. It's inhuman! To suffer like a dog and wake up in chains instead of finding help or care. It is truly insane!"

"I am no madman," said Stres, "as I think you will have occasion to find out."

"But what you're doing is pure madness," the man in shackles replied in the same stentorian voice. "At least accuse me of something plausible. Say that I stole something or killed someone. But don't come and tell me, You travelled on horseback with a woman. As if that was a crime! I would have done better to admit it from the outset, then you would all have been satisfied: yes, I travelled on horseback with a woman. And what of it? What's wrong with that? But I am an honest man, and if I did not say it, it is because I am not in the habit of lying. I intend to lodge a complaint about this wherever I can. I'll go to your prince himself. Higher still if need be, to Constantinople!"

Stres stared at him. The fettered man bore his scrutiny calmly.

"Well," said Stres, "be that as it may, once again I ask you the question you find so insane. This will be the last time. Think carefully before you answer. Did you bring a young woman named Doruntine Vranaj here from Bohemia or from any other far-off place?"

"No," the prisoner replied firmly.

"Wretch," said Stres, turning his eyes from the man. "Put him to the torture," he ordered.

The man's eyes widened in terror. He opened his mouth to speak or to scream, but Stres charged out of the dungeon. As he followed a guard carrying a lantern up the stairs, he quickened his pace so as not to hear the prisoner's cries.

A few minutes later he was on his way home, alone. The rain had stopped, but the path was dimpled with puddles. He let his boots splash in the water as he strode along distractedly. It's dark, you know, I can't see anything, he muttered to himself, repeating the words of the seller of icons.

He thought he heard a voice in the distance, but it was a barking that moved farther away and faded little by little, like ripples on water, in the expanse of the night.

It must be foggy, he thought, or the shadows would not be so deep.

He thought he heard that voice again, and even the muffled sound of footsteps. He started and looked back. Now he could make out the gleam of a lantern swaying in the distance, lighting the broken silhouette of a man in its wan glow. He stopped. The lantern and the splashing of the puddles, which seemed to rise up from a nightmare, were still quite far off when he first heard the voice. He cupped his hand to his ear, trying to make out the words. There were *uhs* and *ehs*, but he heard nothing more distinct. When the man with the lantern had finally come closer, Stres called out.

"What is it?"

"He has confessed," the man answered, breathless. "He has confessed!"

He has confessed, Stres repeated to himself. So those were the words that had sounded to him like *uhs* and *ehs*. He has confessed!

Stres, still motionless, waited until the messenger reached him. He was breathing hard.

"God be praised, he has confessed," the messenger said again, waving his lantern as if to make his words more understandable. "Scarcely had he seen the instruments of torture when he broke down."

Stres looked at him blankly.

"Are you coming back? I'll light the way. Will you question him now?"

Stres did not answer. In fact, that was what the regulation called for. You were supposed to interrogate the prisoner immediately after his confession, while he was still exhausted, without giving him time to recover. And it was the middle of the night, the best time.

The man with the lantern stood two paces away, still panting.

I must not let him recover, Stres said to himself. Of course. Don't allow him even an instant of respite. Don't let him collect himself. That's right, he thought, that's exactly right as far as he's concerned, but what about me? Don't I too need to recover my strength?

And suddenly he realised that the interrogation of the prisoner might well be more trying for him than for the suspect.

"No," he said, "I won't interrogate him tonight. I need some rest." And he turned his back on the man with the lantern.

The next morning, when Stres went down to the cell with his aide, he detected what he thought was a guilty smile on the prisoner's face.

"Yes, truly I would have done better to confess from the start," he said before Stres could ask him a single question. "That's what I had thought to do, in any case, for after all I have committed no crime, and no one has ever yet been condemned for travelling or wandering about in a woman's company. Had I told the truth from the beginning, I would have spared myself this torture, and instead of lying in this dungeon, I would have been at home, where my family is waiting for me. The problem is that once I found myself caught up in this maelstrom of lies – unwittingly, quite by chance – I couldn't extricate myself. Like a man who, after telling some small, inoffensive lie, sinks deeper and deeper instead of taking it back right away, I too believed that I could escape this vexed affair by inventing things which, far from delivering me from my first lie, plunged me further into it. It was all the ruckus about this young woman's journey that got me into this mess. So let me repeat that if I did not confess at once it was only because when I realised what a furore this whole story had caused, and how deeply it had upset everyone, I suddenly felt like a child who has shifted some object the moving of which is a frightful crime in the eyes of the grownups. On the morning of that day – I'll tell you everything in detail in just a minute – when I saw that the homecoming of this young woman had been so, so – how shall I put it? – so disturbing to everyone, especially when everyone suddenly started running around so feverishly asking 'Who was she with?' and 'Who brought her back?', my instinct was to slip away, to get myself out of the whole affair, in which my role, after all, was in any event quite accidental. And that is what I tried to do. Anyway, now I'll tell you the whole story from the beginning. I think you want to know everything, in detail, isn't that right, officer?"

Stres stood, as if frozen, near the rough wooden table.

"I'm listening," he said. "Tell me everything you think you ought to."

The suspect seemed a little uneasy at Stres's indifferent air.

"I don't know, this is the first time I've ever been interrogated, but from what I've heard, the investigator is supposed to ask questions first, then the prisoner answers, isn't that how it works? But you . . ."

"Tell me what you have to say," Stres said. "I'm listening."

The prisoner shifted on his pile of straw.

"Are your shackles bothering you?" Stres asked. "Do you want me to have them taken off?"

"Yes, if that's possible."

Stres motioned to his deputy to release him.

"Thank you," said the prisoner.

He seemed even less self-assured when his hands were freed, and he looked up at Stres once more, still hoping that he would be questioned. But once he realised that his hope was futile, he began speaking in a low voice, his earlier liveliness gone.

"As I told you yesterday, I am an itinerant seller of icons, and it was because of my trade that I happened to make the acquaintance of this young woman. I am from Malta, but I spend most of the year on the road in the Balkans and other parts of Europe. Please stop me if I'm giving you too much detail, for as I said, this is my first interrogation and I'm not sure of the rules. Anyway, I sell icons, and you can well imagine the taste women have for these objects. That was how I came to meet this woman Doruntine in Bohemia one day. She told me that she was a foreigner, originally from Albania, that she had married into a Bohemian family. When I mentioned that I had spent some time in her country, she could not contain her emotion. She said that I was the first person from there that she had met. She asked whether I had any news about what was happening there, whether some calamity had occurred, for none of her family had come to see her. I had heard talk of a war or a plague – in any case a scourge of some kind that had ravaged your country – and after telling her that, I added, hoping to set her mind at rest, that it had happened a long time ago, nearly three years before. Then she cried out, saying: 'But it is exactly three years since I have had any news! Oh woe is me! Surely something terrible must have happened!' Then, overcome, her voice broken by sobs, she told me that she had married a man from this land three years before, that her mother and brothers had not approved of her marrying so far away, but that one of her brothers, whose name was Kostandin, had insisted on it. He had given his mother his word, his *besa*, as you Albanians now call one's pledged word – though it was from her lips that I first heard the expression – promising to bring her daughter back from that far country whenever she wanted him to; that weeks and months had passed, and then years, but no one from her family had come to see her, not even Kostandin, and she missed them so much she couldn't bear it, she felt so alone there among foreigners, and what with missing them so much and feeling so alone, she had begun to feel great anxiety that some catastrophe had happened at home. And since I had told her that there had in fact been a war or a plague, she was sure that something terrible had happened, that her forebodings were well founded. Then she said that she had been thinking of going to see her family herself, but she could not disobey her husband who, though he had promised to take her there, since her brothers seemed to have forsaken her, was too busy with his own affairs to undertake such a long journey.

"As I listened to her speak – in tears she looked even more beautiful – I was suddenly gripped by such a violent desire for her that without a moment's thought I said that if she agreed I could take her to her family myself. My trade has accustomed me to long journeys, and I told her that as simply as if I had offered to take her to the next town, but she thought the idea mad. It was only natural for it to seem insane to her at first, yet curiously, the passion with which she initially rejected my proposal gave me hope, for I had the impression that her protest was meant not so much to persuade me that the idea was really insane as to convince herself. The more she said, 'You're mad, and I am madder still for listening to you,' the more I felt my desire increase, along with my hope that she would yield. So on the next day, when, after a sleepless night, she told me – pale, her voice dull – that she did not see what she could say to her husband if she agreed to come with me, I told myself that I had won. I was convinced that the main thing was to set out alone with her on the roads of Europe. After that, God would provide! Nothing else seemed to matter. I suggested that we didn't have to tell him, for at bottom it was he who was forcing her to act in that way. Had she herself not told me that he had promised to take her to her mother, but that he was kept from doing so by his business? All she had to do, then, was to leave without telling him anything. 'But how can I, how can I?' she asked feverishly. 'How can I explain it to him afterwards? Alone with a stranger!' And she blushed. Of course not, I said, you cannot tell him that you made the journey with a stranger, God forbid! 'Then what can I do?' she asked. And I told her: 'I've thought about it, and what you must do is leave him a letter saying that your brother came to fetch you in great haste, for misfortune has befallen your family.' 'What misfortune?' she interrupted. 'You, stranger, you know what it is, but you don't want to tell me. Oh, my brother must be dead, otherwise he would have come to see me!'

"Two days passed and still she hesitated. I was afraid of being found out and tried to meet her secretly. My desire became uncontrollable. At last she agreed. It was a gloomy late afternoon when she came in haste to the crossroads where I had told her that I would wait for her one last time. I helped her to the crupper and we set off without a word. We rode for a long time, until we felt that we were far enough away that they would not be able to trace us. We spent the night in an out-of-the-way inn and set off again before dawn. I need hardly tell you that she was in a constant state of anxiety. I comforted her as well as I could, and we pressed on. We spent the second night in another inn even farther off the beaten track than the first, in a region I don't even know the name of. I'll spare you the details of my attempts to win her favours. Her pride, and especially her constant anxiety, held her back. But I used every means, from passionate entreaty to threats to abandon her, to leave her alone on the high plateaus of Europe. And so, on the fourth night she gave in. I was so drunk with passion, so giddy, that by the next morning I hardly knew where we were or where we were going. If I am giving useless detail, please stop me. We spent several strange days and nights. We slept in inns that we passed on the way, then we took up our journey again. We sold some of her jewels to pay our expenses. I wanted the journey to last as long as possible, but she was impatient. The closer we came to the Albanian border, the greater was her anxiety. 'What could have happened there?' she asked from time to time. 'What of that war, that plague?' We asked often at the inns, but received only evasive answers. There had indeed been talk of great conflict in Albanian territory, but the reports differed about when it had happened. Some said it had not been war, but plague; others held that the disease hadn't stricken Albania, but some more distant land. Meanwhile, as we neared the Albanian border, the answers grew more definite. Without telling her, I tried to find out more while she rested at the inns. Here everyone knew that war and plague had allied themselves, and had decimated the men of Albania. Once we were in the country's northern principalities, we tried to avoid the major roads and inns, travelling mostly by night. We had now reached the principalities neighbouring her own, and she insisted that we do nothing to call attention to ourselves. We cut across fallow fields, often leaving the roads altogether. We made love wherever we could. In one of the few inns in which we were forced to take shelter from foul weather, I learned the terrible truth about her brothers. Everyone was talking about the great sorrow that had befallen that illustrious house. All her brothers were dead, Kostandin among them. The innkeeper knew the whole story. I began to fear that she would be recognised. As we came closer to her home, we strained our wits to find some acceptable explanation for her arrival. Believing her brothers still alive, she was more frightened than she need have been, whereas for me, knowing the truth as I did, things seemed simpler. In any event, it was easier to account to an old woman stunned by misfortune than to nine brothers.

"She was beside herself in her anxiety about what she could say to her brothers and her mother to explain her arrival. What would she answer when they asked her, 'Who brought you back?' Would she tell the truth? Would she lie? And, if so, what would she say?

"So I found myself compelled to tell her a part of the truth; that is, of the terrible misfortune. I gave her to understand that her brother Kostandin, the one who had promised to bring her back, had died, together with some of his brothers.

"You can well imagine that she went mad with grief, but neither the fatigue of the journey nor her sorrow lessened her worry over the explanation she would have to give for her sudden arrival. It was I who had the idea of explaining her journey in terms of some supernatural intervention. Though I racked my brain, I could find no better explanation. 'There is no other way,' I told her. 'You have to repeat the lie you've already used with your husband. You'll say that Kostandin brought you back.' 'But I was able to lie to my husband,' she replied, 'because he believed my brother was still alive. How can I say the same thing about someone they know is dead?' 'But it'll be even easier,' I told her, 'just because he isn't alive. You'll say that it was your brother who brought you, and they can take it any way they like. What I mean is, they have only to imagine that it was his ghost who brought you back. After all, didn't he promise that, dead or alive, he would fetch you? Everyone knows the exact words of his promise, and they will believe you.'

"Since I knew that her mother alone was still alive, I found the matter quite simple, but she, thinking as she did that at least half of her brothers were alive, scarcely hoped to be believed. But, like it or not, she had to yield to my reasoning. There was no other way. We had no time to think of a more plausible explanation, and in any case neither of us was thinking clearly by then.

"And so, the last night came, the night of 11 October, if I am not mistaken, when, slipping through the darkness like ghosts, we came up to the house. I won't try to tell you about her state of mind – I couldn't describe it. It was past midnight. As we had decided, I stood out of sight, hiding in the half-darkness as she approached the door. But she was in no condition to walk. So I had to lead her to the door where, her hand trembling, she knocked, or more accurately she rested her hand on the knocker, for it was I in fact who moved her hand, cold as a corpse's. I wanted to run off at once, but she was terrified and wouldn't let go of me. In order to calm her, I stroked her hair with my other hand one last time, but at that instant, God be praised, she not only let go but pushed me away in terror. I heard the old woman's voice from behind the door: 'Who is it?' then her answer: 'Open, Mother, it's me, Doruntine,' then the old woman's voice again: 'What did you say?' I had moved away and could not hear the other words clearly, the more so because they were increasingly faint and interrupted with exclamations.

"I made my way back to the highway, to the place where I had left my horse and, mounting, I wandered awhile looking for shelter for the night. We had agreed to meet secretly in two days, but at that point I knew that I would never see her again. The next day and in the days that followed, as I saw the turmoil caused by her arrival, I became convinced not only that I would never see her again but that I had better leave these parts as quickly as possible. I had in the meantime heard of the orders you had issued, and was sure that I was guilty of something impious which, however unaware of it I may have been, might cost me dear indeed. I wanted to slip away as quickly as possible, but how? All the inns, all the relay stations, had been alerted to arrest me on sight. At first I thought of turning myself in and confessing: yes, it was I who brought this woman back, forgive me if I did something wrong, but if

I did, it was without realising it. Then I changed my mind. Why take such a risk? With a bit of skill I could evade the traps that were set for me and be quit of the whole affair. Yet I had a premonition that the honeymoon I had spent with that young woman would turn out to be deadly poisonous. I moved about very cautiously, far from the roads and inns, and mostly by night, like a fox in the woods, as people say. A thousand pardons, I'm getting lost in pointless details again . . . I thought that if I could cross the border of your principality I would be out of danger. I didn't know that the neighbouring principalities and counties had also been notified. And that's how I came to grief. I caught a cold while fording a stream by the baneful name of *Ujana e keqe* – I think that was the name, the 'Evil Uyana' – and I am not quite sure what happened to me next. I was burning with fever, and I remember nothing until I came to and found myself bound hand and foot in an inn. And that's it, Captain. I don't know if I have explained everything properly, but you can ask me any detail at all, and I'll tell you everything. I'm sorry that I didn't behave as I should have from the very beginning, but I hope you'll understand my situation. I'll do everything I can to make amends by answering all your questions honestly."

At last he fell silent, and he sat unblinking under Stres's inspection. His mouth was dry, but he dared not ask for water. Stres stared at him for a long moment. Then, as he opened his mouth to speak, a smile crossed his face like a flash of lightning.

"Is that the truth?" Stres asked.

"Yes, Captain. The whole truth."

"Oh?"

"Yes. The whole truth, Captain."

Stres rose and, his neck stiff as a board, slowly turned his head towards his deputy and the two guards.

"Put him to the torture," he ordered.

Not only the prisoner, but the three other men as well, stiffened in astonishment.

"Torture?" asked his deputy, as though afraid he had misunderstood.

"Yes," said, Stres, his tone icy. "Torture. And don't look at me like that. I know what I'm doing."

He turned on his heels, but at that instant, behind him, the prisoner began to scream, "Captain, no! No! My God, what is this? Why, why?"

Stres climbed the stairs quickly, but he still heard the clanking of the chains with which they secured the prisoner, and his cries as well, which were no less poignant for being muffled.

Stres returned to his office, took up a pencil and began drafting a report for the prince's chancellery:

Report on the arrest of the man who brought back Doruntine Vranaj

Last night Captain Gjikondi of the border detachment delivered to me the man suspected of having brought Doruntine back. In the first interrogation he admitted nothing and denied even knowing a woman by that name, much less having travelled with her. Then, under the threat of torture, he confessed everything, finally throwing light on the mystery of this affair. The events seem to have happened in this manner: at the end of September of this year the man, finding himself in Bohemia in the course of his peregrinations as a seller of icons, made the acquaintance of D. V., and hearing her express her despair at having had no news of her family, promised to take her to her parents' home. He persuaded her to lie to her husband and to write him a letter saying that she had left with her brother Kostandin. The two of them then left Bohemia. On the way he managed to seduce her. At the conclusion of this trying journey, after revealing to her that her brother Kostandin was long dead and finding no other lie with which to justify the journey she had just made with a stranger, he persuaded her to tell her mother that she had been brought back by the ghost of her dead brother, who had thereby fulfilled the promise he had made while he was alive. Subsequently, taking fright, he tried to flee unnoticed and was finally arrested, under circumstances that are well known to you, in the neighbouring county, in an establishment called the Inn of the Two Roberts. He is now being held, on my orders, in complete isolation. I await your instructions on the measures to be taken in this case.

Captain Stres

Of the torture he had ordered inflicted on the prisoner down below in the basement, Stres said not a word. He closed the envelope carefully, sealed it, and instructed a courier to set out at once to deliver it to the capital of the principality. A more or less identical letter was sent to the archbishop at the Monastery of the Three Crosses, with a notice asking that it be forwarded to him in the capital if necessary.

CHAPTER SIX

It had started snowing again, but this snow was different from the last, somehow closer to the world of men. That which was meant to be whitened was whitened, and that which was fated to stay dark remained so. The first icicles hung from the eaves, some of the rivulets had frozen as usual, and the layer of ice was just strong enough to support the weight of the birds. It soon appeared that this would be one of those winters the earth could live with.

Under roofs weighed down by their heavy burden the people talked of Doruntine. By now everyone knew of the arrest of the man who had brought her back, and though they had heard only bits and pieces of the tale he had told, it was enough to cover the world with words, just as a handful of wheat can sow a field.

Many were the messengers who fanned out from the capital through the province during those days, while others, equally numerous, were dispatched from the province to the capital. It was said that a great assembly was being prepared, at which all the rumours and agitation aroused by the alleged resurrection of one of the Vranaj brothers would be laid to rest once and for all. Stres was said to be preparing a detailed report to be presented at the meeting. He had kept the prisoner in isolation, his whereabouts unknown, safe from prying eyes and ears.

Those snippets of the prisoner's confession that had somehow leaked out were now spreading far and wide, carried by word of mouth on puffs of steam in the winter air and borne by carriage from road to road and inn to inn. People travelled less than usual because of the cold, but strangely, the rumours spread just as fast as they would have in more clement weather. It was as if, hardened to crystalline brilliance by the winter frost, they could flow more surely than the rumours of summer, for they were unimpeded by damp and suffocating heat, by the numbing of minds and the jangling of nerves. But that did not prevent them from changing daily as they spread, from swelling, from becoming lighter or darker. And as if all this were not enough, there were still those who said, "Just wait, even stranger things will come." Others, drifting off, would simply sigh, "What next, Lord, what next?"

Everyone awaited the great assembly at which the whole affair would be sifted through in minute detail. The arrival of many nobles from all the principalities of Albania was announced. Rumour had it that the prince himself would attend. Other voices whispered that high church dignitaries from Byzantium would participate, while others, less numerous, even suggested that the Patriarch himself would come in person.

In fact, contrary to what might have been expected, echoes of the Doruntine affair had spread far indeed. The news had even reached Constantinople, capital of the Orthodox religion, and everyone was aware that such things were never pardoned in that city. The highest ecclesiastical authorities were worried, people said. The Emperor himself had been apprised of the incident, which had given him sleepless nights. The issue had proven far more scandalous than it had seemed at first. It was not a simple case of a ghostly apparition, nor even one of those typical calumnies that the Church had always punished with the stake and always would. No, this was far more serious, something that, may God protect us, was shaking the Orthodox religion to its foundations. It concerned the coming of a new messiah – in God's name, lower your voice! – yes, a new messiah, for one man alone had been able to rise from his grave, and that was Jesus Christ, and whosoever affirmed this new resurrection was thereby guilty of an unpardonable sacrilege: belief in a new resurrection, which was tantamount to admitting that there could be two Jesus Christs, for if one believed that someone today had succeeded in doing what Jesus had done in His time, then it was but one small step to admitting – may God preserve us! – that this someone else might be His rival.

Not for nothing had Rome, in its hostility, paid the most careful attention to the development of the case. The Catholic monks had surely outdone themselves in propagating this fable of Kostandin's resurrection, thereby attempting to deal the Orthodox religion a mortal blow by accusing it of *bi-Christicism*, which was a monstrous heresy. Things had got so tense that there was now talk of a universal war of religion. Some even hinted that the impostor who had brought Doruntine back was himself an agent of the Roman Church entrusted with just that mission. Others went further still, claiming that Doruntine herself had fallen into Catholic clutches and had agreed to do their bidding. O great God above, people intoned, may it not be our lot to hear such things! That is how entangled the case had become. But the Orthodox Church of Byzantium, which had spared neither patriarchs nor emperors for infractions of this magnitude, had finally taken the matter in hand and would clear it all up soon enough. The enemies of the Church would be utterly routed.

So said some. Others shook their heads. Not because they disagreed, but because they suspected that the rumour of Kostandin's return from the grave might well have been generated not by the intrigues and rivalry of the world's two major religions but by one of those mysterious disturbances which, like a wicked wind, periodically plague the minds of men, robbing them of judgement, numbing them, and driving them thus dazed and blinded beyond life and death. For life and death, as they saw it, enveloped man in endless successive concentric layers, so that just as there was death within life, so death ought to contain life, which in turn contained death; or perhaps life, itself enveloped in death, harboured death in turn, and so on to infinity. Enough, objected the first group: forget the hair-splitting ratiocination, just say what you mean. The others then sought to explain their point of view more clearly, talking fast lest a mist descend upon their reasoning once more. This alleged resurrection of Kostandin, they said, was in no sense real, and the hoax had been born not at that churchyard grave but in the minds of the people, who, it seemed, had been somehow gripped by a powerful yearning to spin this tale of the mingling of life and death, just as they are sometimes gripped by collective madness. This yearning had cropped up in scattered places, with one, then with another; it had infected them all, so as to turn, at last – abomination of abominations – into a common desire of the quick and the dead to give themselves over to this collective outburst. Short-sighted as they were, people gave no real thought to the abomination they had wrought, for though it is true that everyone feels the urge to see their dead once more, that longing is ephemeral, always arising after some time of turmoil (*Something stopped me from kissing him*, Doruntine had said). If the dead ever really came back and sat before us big as life, you'd see just how terrifying it would be. You think it's difficult to get along with a nonagenarian? Well, imagine dealing with a 900-year-old!

Kostandin's presence, too, like that of any other dead man returned to the land of the living, would be welcome for no more than the briefest lapse of time (*You go on, I have something to do at the church*), for his dead life's proper place was there, in the grave. They say there was a time when dead and living, men and gods, all lived together and sometimes even intermarried, engendering hybrid creatures. But that was an era of barbarism that would never return.

Others listened to these morbid words but preferred to look at matters more simply. If this was all some yearning for resurrection, they said, why bother trying to decide whether it was good or ill? God, after all, would set the date of the Apocalypse, and none save He was entitled to pass judgement on the matter, and still less to decree its advent. But that, others replied, is exactly what's wrong with this rumour of Kostandin's resurrection. The alleged resurrection is taken as a sign that the Apocalypse could occur without an order from the Lord. And the Roman Church accuses ours of having sanctioned this travesty. Now, however, everything will be put right. The Church of Byzantium will not be found wanting. Stres had finally unmasked the great hoax, and the whole country – nay, the whole world, from Rome to Constantinople – would soon learn the truth. Stres would surely be awarded high honours for his achievement.

The light in his window was the last to go out each night. He must be preparing his report. Who can say what we're going to find out, everyone repeated. Blessed are the deaf! In times like these, they are the only people who can sleep soundly.

The sky, though low, seemed particularly distant. Boorishly blocking the view of all four points of the compass, it made not only the old folk but everyone else too complain of the crushing humidity.

But that did not stop them from gossiping. Every day brought new chapters to the story of Doruntine, or else erased parts of it. Only the mourners remained steadfast in their ritual. On the day of the dead, as people made the traditional visits to the graves of their relatives, these women mourned the Vranaj with the very same songs they had sung before:

> Woe betide thee, Kostandin!
> What have you done with your word?
> Does it lie in the grave as you do?

Stres listened to all this talk with an enigmatic smile. He had stopped railing at the old crones or calling them snakes with forked tongues. He'd grown paler of late, but pallor quite suited his looks in winter.

"What exactly does the *besa* mean to you?" he would ask of Kostandin's companions – having recently found pleasure in their company.

The young men looked at one another. There were four of them: Shpend, Milosao, and the two Radhen boys. Stres met them nearly every afternoon at the New Inn, where they used to pass the time when Kostandin was alive. People shook their heads in wonder when they saw Stres with them. Some said that he befriended them as a matter of official duty. Others maintained that he was just killing time. He has finished his report, they said, and now he's taking time off. Others simply shrugged. Who knows why he spends his time with them? He's deep as a well, that Stres. You can never guess why he does one thing rather than another.

"So, what does *besa* mean to you? Or rather, what did it mean to him, to Kostandin?"

None had been more deeply moved by Kostandin's death than these four young men. He had been more than a brother to them, and even now, three years after his death, so strong was his presence in their words and thoughts that many people, half-seriously, half-jokingly, called them "Kostandin's disciples". They looked at one another again. Why was Stres asking them this question?

They had not accepted the captain's company with good grace. Even when Kostandin was alive they had been cool towards him, but in the past few months, as Stres laboured to unravel the mystery of Doruntine's return, the chill had turned icy, bordering on hostility. Stres's first efforts to win them over had run up against this wall. But then, surprisingly, their attitude had changed completely so that they accepted the captain's presence. Young people today are not stupid, was the popular comment at church on Sunday; they know what they're doing.

"It's a term that was used in olden days," Stres went on, "but the meaning attached to it nowadays seems to me more or less new. It has come up more than once in trial proceedings."

They pondered in silence. During their afternoons and evenings with Kostandin, so different from the morose sessions that were now their lot, they had discussed many subjects with great passion, but the *besa* had always been their favourite topic. And for good reason, too: it was a sort of fulcrum, the theme on which all the rest was based.

They had begun to weigh their words with greater care after the bishop issued warnings to all their families. But that was before Kostandin's death. What would they do now that the man they had loved so much was gone? Stres seemed to be familiar with their ideas already; that being the case, all he really had to do was sit and listen. After all, they weren't afraid to express their views. On the contrary, given the opportunity, they were prepared to proclaim them quite openly. What they feared was that their views might be distorted.

"What did Kostandin think about the *besa*?" said Milosao, repeating Stres's question. "It was part of his more general outlook. It would be difficult to explain it without showing its connection with his other convictions."

And they set about explaining everything to him in detail. Kostandin, as the captain must surely know, was an oppositionist, a dissident, as were they, come to that. He was opposed to existing laws, institutions, decrees, prisons, police and courts, which he considered no more than a pack of coercive rules raining down on man like hail. He believed that these laws ought to be abolished and replaced by laws arising from within man himself. By this he did not mean purely spiritual standards dependent on conscience alone, for he was no naive dreamer who assumed that humanity could be ruled solely by conscience. He believed in something far more tangible, something the seeds of which he had detected scattered here and there in Albanian life in recent times, something he said should be nurtured, encouraged to blossom into a whole system. In this system there would be no further need for written laws, courts, jails or police. This new order, of course, would not be wholly free of tragedy, of murder and violence, but man himself would judge his neighbour and be judged by him quite apart from any rigid judicial structure. He would kill or be executed, he would imprison himself or leave prison, when he thought it appropriate.

"But how could such an order be achieved?" asked Stres. Didn't it still come down to conscience in the end, and did not they themselves consider it merely a dream?

They replied that in this new world, existing institutions would have been replaced by immaterial and invisible rules that were nonetheless not at all chimerical or idyllic. In fact they would be rather bleak and tragic, and therefore as weighty as the old ones, if not more so. Except that they would lie within man, not in the form of remorse or some similar sentiment, but as a well-defined ideal, a faith, an order understood and accepted by everyone, but realised within each individual, not secret but revealed for all the world to see, as if man's breast were transparent and his greatness or anguish, his pain, his tragedy, his decisions and doubts, were plainly visible. These were the main lines of an order of this kind. The *besa* was one of them, perhaps the principal one.

Stres butted in to remind them politely that this was quite at odds with the ancient *kanun* the Albanians had inherited from their Illyrian ancestors, whose customary laws, as everyone knew, had been very similar to those of the Ancient Greeks, who had given them the very word *kanun*. Just a year ago he'd read a stage play written by a Greek fifteen hundred years before, and he had been stunned by it . . .

They knew all this, just as they knew that law courts had superseded the *kanun* long before. But they thought that humankind had been inadequately prepared for the transition. They reckoned that in their own era it was more appropriate to renovate the old *kanun* than to adopt a new system of government. The *besa* was a good example . . .

It was still very rare: delicate, like a wild flower needing tender care, its shape as yet undefined. To illustrate their thesis, they reminded Stres of an incident that had occurred some years before, when Kostandin was still alive. In a village not far off, a man had killed his guest. Stres had heard talk of the case. It was then that the expression "He violated the *besa*" had been used. Everyone in the village, young and old, had been deeply shaken by the event. Together they decided that no such disgrace would ever befall them again. In fact they went further still, decreeing that anyone, known or unknown, who entered the territory of their village would stand under the protection of the *besa* and would thereby be declared a friend and be protected as such, that the doors of the village would be opened to anyone, at any hour of the night or day, and that any passer-by must be given food and his safety assured. In the marketplace of the capital they were the butt of jokes. Anyone want a free meal? Just head for that village and knock on any door; talk about consideration, they'll escort you to the village border as if you were a bishop. But the villagers, ignoring the mockery, went even further. They requested – and received – the prince's permission to punish those who violated the *besa*. No one guilty of such an offence could leave the territory of the village alive. Another village, quite far from the first, asked the prince to grant them the same right, on terms that were no less curious: the villagers requested that protection of their *besa* cover not only their own place of habitation, but also a sector of the highway, including two inns and a mill. But the prince was afraid that if he allowed the new rule to spread it would interfere with traffic along the highway and complicate the administration of that part of the country, and so he refused.

That was what the *besa* meant. That was how Kostandin saw it. He considered the *besa* a bond linking all that was sublime, and he felt that once it and other similar laws had spread and held sway in every aspect of life, then external laws, with their corresponding institutions, would be shed naturally, just as a snake sloughs off its old skin.

Thus spoke Kostandin on those memorable afternoons they used to pass at the New Inn, where he went on and on about *Albanianness*. Perorating, or as some wits put it, *albanating*. "So that's how it is," he would say, "for my part, I shall give my mother my *besa* to bring Doruntine back to her from her husband's home whenever she desires. And whatever happens – if I am lying on my deathbed, if I have but one hand or one leg, if I have lost my sight, even if . . . I will never break that promise."

"Even if . . . ?" Stres repeated. "Tell me, Milosao, don't you think he meant 'even if I'm dead'?"

"Perhaps," the young man answered absently, looking away.

"But how can you account for that?" Stres asked. "He was an intelligent man, he didn't believe in ghosts. I have a report from the bishop stating that at Easter you and he laughed at people's faith in the resurrection of Christ. So how could he have believed in his own resurrection?"

They looked at one another, each suppressing a smile.

"You are right, Captain, so long as you are speaking of the present world, the existing world. But you must not forget that he, that all of us, in our words and thoughts, had in mind another world, one with a new dimension, a world in which the *besa* would reign supreme. In that world everything could be different."

"Nevertheless, you live in our world, in this existing world," said Stres.

"Yes. But a part of our being, perhaps the best part, lies in the other."

"In the other," he repeated softly. He was now the only one suppressing a smile.

They took no notice of it, or pretended not to, and went on discussing Kostandin's other ideas, the reasons why he held that this reorganisation of life in Albania was necessary. These had to do with the great storms he saw looming on the horizon and with Albania's location, caught in a vice between the religions of Rome and Byzantium, between two worlds, West and East. Their clash would inevitably bring appalling turmoil, and Albania would have to find new ways to defend itself. It had to create structures more stable than "external" laws and institutions, eternal and universal structures lying within man himself, inviolable and invisible and therefore indestructible. In short, Albania had to change its laws, its administration, its prisons, its courts and all the rest, it had to fashion them so that they could be severed from the outside world and anchored within men themselves as the tempest drew near. It had to do this imperatively or it would be wiped from the face of the earth. Thus spoke Kostandin. And he held that this new organisation would begin with the *besa*.

"Then of course," Stres said, "Kostandin's own default, the violation of his promise, was all the more serious and inadmissible, was it not?"

"Oh yes, certainly. Especially after his mother's curse. Except for one thing, Captain Stres: there was no default. He kept his promise in the end. Somewhat belatedly, of course, but he had a good enough reason for being late: he was dead. In the end he kept his word in spite of everything."

"But he was not the one who brought Doruntine back," said Stres. "You know that as well as I do."

"For you, perhaps, it wasn't him. We see it differently."

"Truth is the same for all. Almost anyone could have brought Doruntine here – except Kostandin!"

"Nevertheless, it was he who brought her back."

"So you believe in resurrection?"

"That's secondary. It has nothing to do with the heart of the matter."

"Just the same, if you don't accept the resurrection of the dead, how can you persist in claiming that he made that journey with his sister?"

"But that is of no importance, Captain Stres. That is completely secondary. The essential thing is that it was he who brought Doruntine here."

"Maybe it's this business about two worlds that prevents us from understanding one another," Stres said. "What is a lie in one may be the truth in the other, is that the idea?"

"Maybe . . . Maybe."

Meanwhile, the country seethed as it awaited the great assembly. Words, calculations, forebodings and news fluttered in the wind like yellowing leaves before a storm, falling to earth only to be raised anew. Drenched in road dirt or whitened by rime, messengers began cropping up all over the place, even while the date of the great assembly remained unknown. Some believed it would happen before Easter, others said straight after. But once folk had become convinced that it would be around Easter time, they claimed it was no coincidence that the Lord had set the date close to that of the Day of Resurrection: he wanted to test their souls one more time, to press them and torture them for who knows what ancient sin.

CHAPTER SEVEN

Turning his head towards the window to see if day had yet broken, Stres noticed a fine blond hair on his pillow. What's that? he wondered, but sleep dragged him down before he could think about it any further.

When he woke up properly later on it was already broad daylight. He looked at his pillow as if trying to find something, then got out of bed noiselessly and went over to the window, where he inspected the catch to check whether or not it had been forced during the night. He could not have said whether he had just imagined Doruntine's grave opening up and her hair waving in the wind or whether he had seen such a thing in a dream. Then he glanced at his pillow again. Really, his nerves must be in a terrible state if it took only a moment for his mind to wander off in such directions. He was so convinced he had seen that hair that he stopped to look at the house over the street, where, a few weeks previously, he had seen a girl brushing her hair at the window. If it had been summertime, and windows had been left open, he could have believed that the wind had just blown one of her hairs into his bedroom.

"Stres?" his wife said, still drowsing. "You're up at the crack of dawn once again. Brrr . . ."

She mumbled something incomprehensible but instead of then burying her head under the pillows as she usually did when her husband woke her up, she propped herself on an elbow and shot him a pitying glance:

"They'll be the death you with their . . . what do you call them . . . with their *conferences*!"

Said by his wife, "conferences" sounded just as foreign to him as the mumbling that had preceded it.

"Conferences," he muttered to himself, as if trying to summon up the word's original meaning. It was an everyday kind of word, but there was an unprecedented air of horror hanging over it now. A horror that, unlike many others, did not spring up from the depths of the past but was prompted by a vision of the future.

Stres kept his eyes on the grey horizon. These days, his mind turned more and more towards the future, but far from giving him any relief, it only made him more distraught.

He left the house an hour later and from outside he glanced up at the window whence the blond hair had perhaps floated, then strode rapidly to his office.

"What's new?" he asked his deputy.

The aide listed the latest events that he had received note of during the night.

"Nothing else?" Stres inquired. "Nothing unusual? No graves profaned? These days anything can happen, can't it?"

His deputy reported that he had received no information about any acts of that kind.

"Really? Well then, take me to the Old Monastery. We'll see how the preparations are coming along."

It was in an inner courtyard of the Old Monastery, large enough to hold some two thousand people, that the great assembly was to be held. Carpenters spent several days setting up wooden grandstands for the guests and a platform from which Stres would speak. Tarpaulins were strung up in case of rain.

The meeting was to take place on the first Sunday in April, but by mid-week most of the region's inns were full, not only those closest to the Old Monastery, but also the ones along the highway. Guests, clergy and laymen alike, poured in from the four corners of the principality and from neighbouring principalities, dukedoms and counties. Visitors were expected from the farthest principalities, and envoys from the Holy Patriarchate in the Empire's capital.

As they watched the carriages parade down the highway – most of their doors decorated with coats of arms, the passengers dressed in gaudy clothes often embroidered with the same coats of arms as those on their coaches – the people, chatting with one another, learned more in those few days about princely courts, ceremonies, dignitaries and religious and secular hierarchies than they had in their whole lifetime. It was only then that they came to realise the full import, the truly enormous significance, of this whole affair, which, at first, on that night of 11 October, had been considered simply a ghost story.

Stres and his deputy went in through an ill-lit side

door. Once the preparations had been completed, the carpenters had gathered up their tools and left. The open stands were wet beneath the steady drizzle. Stres went up to the podium where he was going to speak and stared at the empty benches.

He stared at them for a long time, then suddenly turned his head sharply right and left, as though someone had called him or he had heard shouts. The hint of a bitter smile crossed his face; then, with long strides, he walked away.

Finally the long-awaited day dawned. It was cold, one of those days that seems all the more icy when you realise it's Sunday. The high clouds were motionless, as if moored to the heavens. From early morning the monastery's inner courtyard was packed with spectators – except for the stands reserved for high-ranking officials and guests – and the innumerable latecomers, hoping to be able to hear something, had no choice but to assemble outside in the empty field that ringed the walls. They had to learn, at all costs, what was said at the gathering, and quickly, for they formed the first circle the news must reach so that it might spread in waves throughout the world.

Bundled up in grey goatskins to protect themselves from the cold and especially the rain, they watched the arrival of the endless procession of horses and carriages from which the invited guests descended. They looked glum already, as if what was about to flood into the arena and invade their very breasts would turn out to be worse than a whirlwind. But no matter. They had all come here to confront a scourge – or else a divine revelation.

In the courtyard the stands were gradually filling up. Last to take their seats were the personal envoy of the prince, the delegates from Byzantium (accompanied by the archbishop of the principality), and Stres, dressed in his black uniform with the deer antler insignia, looking taller, but also paler, than usual.

The archbishop left the group of guests and walked towards the podium, apparently to open the meeting. A wave of shushing among the crowd allowed silence to settle gradually over the great courtyard. Only when it had become almost complete was that silence broken by a rumbling that had hitherto been inaudible. It was the noise of the crowd outside the monastery walls.

The archbishop tried to speak in a strong, loud voice, but outside the vaulted dome of his cathedral he could not make his voice really boom. He seemed annoyed at the feebleness of his diction and cleared his throat, but his tone was muffled mercilessly by the vastness of the court-yard whose walls, had they not been so low, might perhaps have given resonance and volume to his eloquence. But the prelate spoke on nonetheless. He briefly mentioned the purpose of this great meeting that had been called to shed light upon the great hoax that had so regrettably been born in this village with "someone's alleged return from the grave and his journey with some living woman." (His intonation of *someone's* and *some* gave his audience to understand that he disdained to cite the names of Kostandin and Doruntine.) He mentioned the spread of this hoax throughout the principality, beyond its borders, and indeed even beyond the confines of Albania; he suggested what unimaginable catastrophes could result if such heresies were permitted to spread freely. And finally he noted the efforts by the Church of Rome to exploit the heresy, using it against the Holy Byzantine Church, as well as the measures taken by the latter to unmask the imposture.

"And now," he concluded, "I yield the platform to Captain Stres, who was entrusted with the investigation of this matter and who will now present a detailed report on all aspects of it. He will explain to you, step by step, how the hoax was conceived; he will tell you who was behind the story of the dead man returned from the grave, what the alleged journey of the sister with her dead brother really was, what happened afterwards, and how the truth was brought to light."

A deep rumbling drowned out his final words as Stres rose from his seat and headed for the platform.

He raised his head, looked out at the crowd and waited for the first layer of silence to fall over it once more. He spoke his first words in a voice that seemed very soft. Little by little, as the crowd's silence grew deeper, it sounded louder. In chronological order he set out the events of the night of 11 October and after; he recalled Doruntine's arrival, her claim to have returned in the company of her dead brother, and his own initial suspicions: that an impostor had deceived Doruntine, that Doruntine herself had lied both to her mother and to him, that the young woman and her partner had hatched the hoax in concert, or even that it was no more than a belated vendetta of some kind, a settling of scores or a struggle for succession. He then reviewed the measures taken to discover the truth, the research into the family archives, the checks on the inns and relay stations, and finally the failure of all these various efforts to shed any light at all on the mystery. Then he recalled the spread of the first rumours, mentioning the mourners, his suspicion that Doruntine had gone mad and that the trip with her brother was no more than the product of a diseased imagination. But at that point, he continued, the arrival of two members of the husband's family had confirmed that the journey had really occurred and that the horseman who had taken Doruntine up behind him had been seen. Stres then described the fresh measures that he and other officials of the principality had been compelled to take in their effort to solve the mystery, measures that led at length to the capture of the impostor – the man who had played the role of the dead brother – at the Inn of the Two Roberts in the next county.

"I interrogated him myself," Stres continued. "At first he denied knowing Doruntine. In fact he denied everything, and it was only when I ordered him put to the torture that he confessed. Here, according to him, is what really happened."

Stres then recounted the prisoner's confession. His every word brought murmurs of relief from the crowd. It was as if they had all been yearning for this bleak story, hitherto so macabre, to be freshened by the gentle breeze of the itinerant merchant's tale of romantic adventure. The rippling murmur breached the monastery walls and spread into the field beyond, just as silence, shuddering and terror in turn had spread before.

"This, then, is what the prisoner stated," Stres said, raising his voice. He paused for a moment, waiting for silence. "It was midnight . . ."

The silence grew deeper, but the murmur rising from

the most distant rows, and especially from ou
walls, was still audible.

"It was midnight when he finished his accoun
it was then that I—"

Here he paused again, in one final effort to unroll the
carpet of silence as far as possible.

"Then, to the astonishment of my aides, I ordered
him put to the torture again."

A sulphurous light seemed to glow in Stres's eyes. He
gazed for a moment at those silent faces, at the darkened
features of the people in the grandstands, and spoke again.

"If I had him put to the torture again, it was because
I doubted the truth of his tale."

Silence still reigned, but Stres thought he felt what
could have been a mild earthquake. Now! he said to
himself, intoxicated, now! Bring it all down!

"He resisted the torture for a week. Then, on the eighth
day, he confessed the truth at last. That is to say, he admitted
that everything he had said until then had been nothing
but lies."

The earthquake, which he had been the first to sense,
had now in fact begun: its roar was rising, a muffled thunder,
out of phase, of course, like any earthquake, but powerful
nonetheless. A lightning glance to his right showed all
was still mute there. But those frozen faces in the grandstands had clouded over entirely.

"It was nothing but a tissue of lies from start to
finish," Stres continued, surprised that he hadn't been interrupted. "The man had never met Doruntine, had never
spoken to her, had neither travelled with her nor made
love to her, any more than he had brought her back on the

night of 11 October. He had been paid to perpetrate the hoax."

Stres raised his head, waiting for something that he himself could not have defined.

"Yes," he went on, "paid. He himself confessed as much; paid by persons whose names I shall not mention here."

He paused briefly once again. The crowd now suddenly seemed very far away. Maybe people's screams could no longer reach him. Or their spears. Or their nails.

"At first," Stres went on, "when this impostor denied knowing Doruntine, he played his role to perfection, and he did equally well afterwards, when he affirmed that in fact he had brought her back. But just as great impostors often betray themselves in small details, so he gave himself away with a trifle. In his attempt to be persuasive, and especially by rejoicing too soon at having achieved his aim, he was led to supply irrelevant details. That his how he tore the mask from his own face. Thus this impostor, this imaginary companion of Doruntine—"

"Then who brought the woman back?" shouted the archbishop from his seat. "The dead man?"

Stres turned towards him.

"Who brought Doruntine back? I will answer you on that very point, for I was in charge of this case. Be patient, Your Eminence, be patient, noble sirs!"

Stres took a deep breath. So many hundreds of lungs swelled along with his that he felt as if all the air about them had been set in motion. Once again he glanced slowly across the packed courtyard to the stands, at the foot of which the guards stood with their arms akimbo.

"I expected that question," said Stres, "and am

therefore prepared to answer it." He paused again. "Yes, I have prepared myself with the greatest care to answer it. The painstaking investigation I conducted is now closed, my file complete, my conviction unshakable. I am ready, noble sirs, to answer the question 'Who brought Doruntine back?'"

Stres allowed yet another brief moment of silence, during which he glanced in all directions as if seeking to convey the truth with his eyes before expressing it with his voice.

"Doruntine," he said, "was in fact brought back by Kostandin."

Stres stiffened, expecting some sound – laughter, jeers, shouts, an uproar of some kind, even a challenging cry: "But for two months you've been trying to convince us of the contrary!" Nothing of the kind came from the crowd.

"Yes, Doruntine was brought back by Kostandin," he repeated as if he feared that he had been misunderstood. But people's stupefaction was evidence enough that his words had reached them. He thought that their silence was perhaps excessive, as it can be in response to fear.

"Just as I promised you, noble sirs, and you, honoured guests, I will explain everything. All I ask is that you have the patience to hear me out."

At that moment Stres's only concern was to keep his mind clear. For the time being he asked for nothing more.

"You have all heard," he began, "some of you before setting out for this gathering, others on your way here or upon your arrival, of the strange marriage of Doruntine Vranaj, the marriage that lies at the root of this whole affair. You are all aware, I imagine, that this far-off marriage, the first to be consummated with a man from so distant a country, would never have taken place if Kostandin, one of the bride's brothers, had not given his mother his word that he would bring Doruntine back to her whenever she desired her daughter's presence, on occasions of joy or sorrow. You also know that not long after the wedding the Vranaj, like all of Albania, were stricken with unspeakable grief. Yet no one brought Doruntine back, for he who had promised to do so was dead. You are aware of the curse the Lady Mother uttered against her son for his violation of the *besa*, and you know that three weeks after that curse was spoken, Doruntine at last appeared at the family home. That is why I now affirm, and reaffirm, that it was none other than her brother Kostandin, in accordance with his oath, his *besa*, who brought Doruntine back. There is no other explanation for that journey, nor could there be. It matters little whether or not Kostandin returned from the grave to accomplish his mission, just as it matters little who was the horseman who set out on that dark night or what horse he saddled, whose hands held the reins, whose feet pressed against the stirrups, whose hair was matted with the highway dust. Each of us has a part in that journey, for it is here among us that Kostandin's *besa* germinated, and that is what brought Doruntine back. Therefore, to be more exact I would have to say that it was all of us – you, me, our dead lying there in the graveyard close by the church – who, through Kostandin, brought Doruntine back."

Stres swallowed.

"Aha!" the archbishop thundered from his seat, "at last you confess to your own part in this abomination!"

"All our parts . . ." Stres said, as he tried to make his meaning clear, but the archbishop's voice overrode his own.

"Speak for yourself!" the prelate yelled. "And by the way, I would really like to know where you were between 30 September and 11 October. Where were you, exactly?"

Stres kept his composure but his face had turned as white as a sheet.

"Answer, Captain!" someone shouted.

"All right, I'll tell you," Stres responded. "During the period alluded to I was on a secret mission."

"Aha! More mysteries!" the archbishop screamed. "So be it! But so we may know the truth of the matter, we would like you to tell us what the mission consisted of."

"It was the kind of job that even we officers seek to forget once it is done. I have nothing to add."

This time the rumbling of the crowd that echoed from the walls took longer to abate. Stres took a deep breath.

"Noble sirs, I have not yet finished. I would like to tell you – and most of all to tell our guests from distant lands – just what this sublime power is that is capable of bending the laws of death."

Stres paused again. His throat felt dry and he found it hard to form his words. But he kept speaking just the same. He spoke of the *besa*, of its spread among the Albanians. As he spoke he saw someone in the crowd coming towards him, holding what seemed to be a heavy object, perhaps a stone. They're already coming, he thought, and with his elbow he touched the pommel of his sword beneath his cloak. But as the man drew nearer, Stres saw that it was one of the Radhen boys, and that he carried not a stone to strike him with, but a small pitcher.

Stres smiled, took the pitcher and drank.

"And now," he went on, "let me try to explain why this new moral law was born and is now spreading among us. The question is this: in these new conditions of the worsening of the general atmosphere in the world, in this time of crime and hateful treachery that could be called *unbelief*, who should the Albanian be? What face shall he show the world? Shall he espouse evil or stand against it? Shall he disfigure himself, changing his features to suit the masks of the age, seeking thus to assure his survival, or shall he keep his countenance unchanged ... I am a servant of the state and have little interest in the personal aspects of Kostandin's journey, if in fact there are any. Each of us, commoners and lords alike, be we Caesar or Christ, is the shroud of unfathomable mysteries. But, functionary that I am, I have spoken of the general point, the one that concerns Albania. Albania's time of trial is near, the hour of choice between these two faces. And if the people of Albania, deep within themselves, have begun to fashion institutions as sublime as the *besa*, that shows us that Albania is making the right choice. Albania aims to keep its eternal image. That's the main thing, to my mind. She will keep her face not by retreating from the world like a wild animal at bay, but by joining the world. It was to carry that message to Albania and to the world beyond that Kostandin rose from his grave."

Once more Stres's glance embraced the numberless crowd that stretched before him, then the stands to his right and left. He thought he saw the gleam of tears here and there. But the people's eyes were, in fact, empty.

"But it is not easy to accept this message," he went

on. "It will require great sacrifices by successive genera-
tions. Its burden will be heavier than the cross of Christ.
And now that I have come to the end of what I had to
tell you" – and here Stres turned to the stands where the
envoys of the prince were seated – "I would like to add
that, since my words are at variance with my duties, or at
least are at variance with them *for the moment*, I now resign
my post."

He raised his right hand to the white antler insignia
sewn on the left side of his cloak and, pulling sharply,
ripped it off and let it fall to the ground.

Without another word he descended the wooden
stairway and, his head held high, walked through the crowd,
which parted at his passing with a mixture of respect and
dread.

From that day forward, Stres was never seen again. No
one, neither his deputies nor his family, not even his wife,
knew where he was – or at least no one would say.

At the Old Monastery the wooden grandstands and
platform were dismantled, porters carried off the planks
and beams, and in the inner courtyard there was no longer
any trace of the assembly. But no one forgot a word that
Stres had spoken there. His words passed from mouth to
mouth, from village to village, with unbelievable speed.
The rumour that Stres had been arrested in the wake of
his speech soon proved unfounded. It was said that he had
been seen somewhere, or at least that someone had heard
the trot of his horse. Others insisted they had caught a
glimpse of him on the northern highway. They were sure
they had recognised him, despite the dusk and the first layer

of dust that covered his hair. Who can say? people mused, who can say? How much, O Lord, must our poor minds take in! And then someone said, his voice trembling as if shivering with cold:

"Sometimes I wonder if he didn't bring Doruntine back himself."

"How dare you say such a thing?"

"What would be so surprising?" the man answered. "As for myself, I have not been surprised by anything since the day she returned."

As was only to be expected, the old dispute over local versus foreign marriages arose once again. Proponents of local marriages now seemed likely to prevail, but the other faction proved obstinate. Each side had its own explanation of the dead man's ride. The distant marriage faction emphasised respect of the *besa* and obviously saw Kostandin as its standard bearer. The other side treated his journey as an act of repentance, in other words as a resurrection intended to make good a fault. A third group, who saw in the man's long ride an attempt to reconcile opposites – distance and proximity – that had torn him apart as much as his incestuous yearnings, was much less prominent.

With the idea of local marriage constantly gaining ground, the sad story of Maria Matrenga was quoted more and more often, despite the fact that, like some predestined counterweight, Palok the Idiot wandered around the village alleyways ever more visibly.

When the poor yokel was found dead one fine morning, people's initial distress was quickly replaced by an understanding that his murderers would never be identified. The incident was accounted for, as many are, in two different ways. Supporters of distant marriages maintained that Palok had been slaughtered by his own kin, that is to say by defenders of local unions, so as to remove from the street this visible evidence that did their cause harm every day of the week. But their adversaries obstinately insisted that the killing had been done by the supporters of exogamy, so as to show that even though their ideals were on the wane, they were still prepared to defend them, even by spilling blood.

All the same, despite this new bone of contention, things proceeded as they always do when a simpleton is killed, for unlike cases where dogs are put down, they often lead to reconciliation. Tension between the two factions went into sharp decline.

While time now seemed to be on the side of local marriages, an event took place which could have seemed ordinary in any other season, but was not at all normal in mid-winter. A young woman of the village married and left to join her husband in some far-off place. Everyone was shocked to hear talk of a new Doruntine at such a time of year. People thought that after the uproar over all that had taken place in the village, the bride's family would break the engagement or at least put off the wedding for a while. But the ceremony took place on the appointed day, the groom's relatives came over from their country, which some people said was six days away, while others said eight. After they had done with all their feasting and drinking and singing of songs, they took the young woman away with them. Almost the entire village walked with them from the church, as they had done years before with sorry Doruntine, and seeing the bride looking so beautiful, almost wraith-like in her white veil, many must have wondered whether on some moonless night some ghost might not go and bring her back home again. But the bride, for her part, astride her white horse, showed not the slightest sign of worry about her fate. People watching her leave nodded their heads, saying, "Good Lord, maybe young brides nowadays like that sort of thing, maybe they like riding at night, hanging on to a shadow, through the dark and the void . . ."

Tirana, October 1979

THE
SIEGE

As winter fell away and the Sultan's envoys departed, we realised that war was our ineluctable fate. They had pressured us in every way to accept being vassals of the Sultan. First they used flattery, promising us a part in governing their vast empire. Then they accused us of being renegades in the pay of the Frankish knights, that is to say, slaves of Europe. Finally, as was to be expected, they made threats.

You seem mighty sure of your fortresses, they said to us, but even if they are as sturdy as you think, we'll throttle you with an altogether more fearsome iron band – hunger and thirst. At each season of harvest and threshing, the only seeded field you'll see will be the sky, and your only sickle the moon.

And then they left. All through March their couriers galloped as fast as the wind bearing messages to the Sultan's Balkan vassals, telling them either to persuade us to give in, or else to cut off all relations with us. As was to be expected, all were obliged to take the latter course.

We were alone and knew that sooner or later they would come. Many times in the past we had faced attacks from our enemies, but lying in wait of the mightiest army the world had ever known was a different matter. Our own minds were perpetually abuzz, but our prince, George Castrioti, was preoccupied beyond easy imagining. The inland castles and coastal keeps were ordered to repair their watchtowers and above all to build up stocks of arms and supplies. We did not yet know from which direction they would come, but in early June we heard that they had begun to march along the old Roman road, the Via Egnatia, so they were heading straight towards us.

One week later, as fate decreed that our castle would be the first defence against the invasion, the icon of the Virgin from the great church at Shkodër was brought to us. A hundred years before it had given the defenders of Durrës the strength to repulse the Normans. We all gave thanks to Our Immaculate Lady and felt calmer and stronger for it.

Their army moved slowly. It crossed our border in mid-June. Two days later George Castrioti came with Count Musaka to inspect the garrison one last time, and to give it his blessing. After issuing final instructions, he left the castle on Sunday afternoon, followed by his escort and the officers' womenfolk and children, so as to place them in safety in the mountains.

We walked alongside them for a while without speaking. Then we made our adieus with much feeling and went back into the keep. From look-outs on our towers we watched them climb up to the Plain of the Cross, then we saw them re-emerge on the Evil Slope and finally disappear into the Windy Ravine. Then we closed the heavy outer doors, and the fortress seemed to have gone mute now that we could no longer hear the voices of our youngsters inside it. We also battened down the inner sets of doors and let silence reign over us.

On June 18, at daybreak, we heard the tolling of the bell. The sentinel on the East Tower announced that a yellowish cloud could be seen in the far distance. It was the dust kicked up by their horses.

CHAPTER ONE

The first Turkish troops came beneath the walls of the fortress on June 18. They spent the day pitching camp. By evening the entire army had still not arrived. New units kept on coming in. A thick layer of dust lay on men, shields, flags and drums, horses and wagons, and on the camels laden with bronze and heavy equipment. As soon as each marching group came on to the plain that lay before the garrison, officers from a special battalion would allocate a specific camping site, and the weary soldiers, under orders from their leaders, would busy themselves with setting up the tents before collapsing inside them, half-dead from fatigue.

Ugurlu Tursun Pasha, the commander-in-chief, stood alone outside his pink pavilion. He was watching the sun set. The huge camp throbbed with the noise of horseshoes and a thousand voices, and with its long lines of tents, it looked to him like a giant octopus which would stretch out one tentacle after another and slowly but surely encircle and suffocate the castle. The nearest tents were less than a hundred paces from the ramparts, the furthest were beyond the horizon. The Pasha's lieutenants had insisted his pavilion be placed at least a thousand paces from the castle walls. But he had refused to be so far away. Some years earlier, when he had been still a young man and of less elevated rank, he had often slept less than fifty paces from the ramparts, almost at the foot of the besieged citadel. Later on, however, in successive wars and sieges, as he rose in rank, the colour of his tent and its distance from the walls had changed in tandem. It was now pitched at a distance slightly more than half of what his lieutenants recommended, that is, at six hundred paces. That was a lot less than a thousand, all the same.

The Pasha sighed. He often did that when he took up quarters before a fortress that had to be taken. It was a reflex prompted by the first impression, always the deepest, before he became accustomed to the situation – it was rather like getting used to a woman. Each of his apprehensions began the same way, and they always also ended with another sigh, a sigh of relief, when he cast his last glance at a vanquished fortress, waiting, like a small and dusky widow, for the order for restoration, or for final demolition.

On this occasion, the citadel that soared up before him looked particularly gloomy, like most of the fortresses of the Christians. There was something odd, or even sinister, in the shape and lay-out of its towers. He had had that same impression two months earlier, when the surveyors responsible for planning the campaign had brought him drawings of the structure. He had spread out the charts on his knees many times, for hours on end, after dinner, when everyone else in his great house at Bursa was sleeping. He knew every detail of the lay-out by heart, and yet, now that he was at last seeing it with his own eyes, it aroused in him a sense of foreboding.

He glanced up at the cross on the top of the citadel's church. Then at the fearsome banner, the two-headed black eagle whose outline he could barely make out. The vertical drop beneath the East Tower, the wasteland around the gallows, the crenellated keep, all these other sights gradually grew dark. He raised his eyes to take another look at the cross, which seemed to him to give off an eerie glow.

The moon had not yet risen. It struck him as rather odd that the Christians, having seen Islam take possession of the moon, had not promptly made their own emblem the sun, but had taken instead a mere instrument of torture, the cross. Apparently they weren't as clever as people claimed. But they had been even less bright in times when they believed in several gods.

The sky was now black. If everything was decided up on high, why did Allah put them through so many trials, why did he allow them to spill so much blood? To one camp He had given ramparts and iron doors to defend itself, and to the other, ladders and ropes to try to overcome them, and He was content just to be a spectator of the ensuing butchery.

But the Pasha didn't rebel against fate and he turned around to look at his own camp. The plain was gradually being drowned in darkness and the myriad white tents appeared to hover above the ground like a bank of fog. He could see the different corps of the army laid out according to the plan that had been agreed. From where he was standing, he could see the snow-white flags of the janissaries, and the copper cauldron they hung on top of a tall pole. The raiders, or *akinxhis*, were taking their horses to drink in the nearby stream. Further on lay the endless tents of the *azabs*, as the infantry units were called; beyond them were the tents of the *eshkinxhis*, the cavalry recruited for this campaign; then, further on still, the tents of the swordsmen known as *dalkiliç*, then the quarters of the *serden geçti*, the soldiers of death, then the *müslüman* or Muslim troops, and the prettier abodes of the *sipahi*, the regular cavalry. Spread out behind them were the Kurdish units, then the Persians, the Tartars, the Caucasians and the Kalmyks, and, even further off, where the commander's eye could no longer make out any clear shapes, there must have been the motley horde of the irregular volunteers, the exact number of whom was known to no man. Everything was gradually falling into order. A large part of the army was already sleeping. The only noise to be heard was the sound of quartermasters unloading supplies from the camel trains. Crates of bronze pieces, cauldrons, innumerable sacks bursting with victuals, gourds of oil and honey, fat cartons full of all kinds of equipment, iron bars, stakes, forks, hempen ropes with hooks on their ends, clubs, whetstones, bags of sulphur, and a whole array of metal tools he could not even name – all now came to rest in growing piles on the ground.

At the moment the army was swathed in darkness but at the crack of dawn it would shimmer like a Persian carpet as it spread itself out in all directions. Plumes, tents, manes, white and blue flags, and crescents – hundreds and hundreds of brass, silver, and silk crescents – would burst into flower. The pageant of colour would make the citadel look even blacker beneath its symbolic instrument of torture, the cross. He had come to the end of the earth to topple that sign.

In the deepening silence the sound of the *azabs* at work on the ditches became more noticeable. He was well aware that many of his officers were cursing through their teeth and hoping that as he was himself half-dead from fatigue he would give the order to halt work on the drains. He clenched his jaw just as he had when he had first spoken about latrines at a meeting of the high command. An army, he said, before it was a marching horde, or a swathe of flags, or blood to be spilled, or a victory or a defeat – an army was in the first place an ocean of piss. They had listened to him open-mouthed as he explained that in many cases an army may begin to fail not on the field of battle, but in mundane details of unsuspected importance, details no one thought about, like stench and filth, for instance.

In his mind's eye he saw the drains moving ever closer to the river, which would wake in the morning looking dull and yellow . . . In fact, that was how war really began, and not as the *hanums* in the capital – the ladies of high society – imagined it.

He almost laughed at the thought of those fine ladies, but oddly, a sense of nostalgia stopped him. It was the first time he'd noticed himself having feelings of that kind. He shook his head as if to make fun of his own plight. Yes, he really did miss the *hanums* of Bursa, but that was only part of it. What he missed was his distant homeland,

Anatolia. He had often thought of its peaceful, lazy plains during the long march through the Balkans. He had thought of it most of all when his army had entered the land of the Shqipetars and first seen its fearsome peaks. One morning before noon, when he was drowsing on horseback, he had heard the cry from all around: "*daglar, daglar*", but said in a special way, as if expressing fear. His officers raised their heads and looked to the left, then to the right, as if they were trying to get a better view. He too gazed at the mountains at length. He'd never seen any like them before. They reminded him of ghastly nightmares unrelieved by waking up. The ground and the rocks seemed to be scrambling madly towards the sky in mockery of the laws of nature. Allah must have been very angry when he created this land, he thought, and for the hundredth time since the start of the campaign he wondered if his leadership of the army had been won for him by his friends, or by his enemies.

In the course of the journey he had noticed that the mere sight of these mountains could make his officers agitated. They spoke more and more often of the plain they hoped to see before them as soon as possible. The army moved slowly, for now it hauled not only its arms and supplies, but also the heavy shadow of the Albanian mountains. The worst of it was that there was nothing he could do to be rid of it. His only resource was to summon the campaign chronicler and to ask him how he was going to describe the mountainous terrain. Trembling with fear, the chronicler had said that in order to portray the Albanian landscape he had assembled a series of terrifying epithets. But they hadn't met with the Pasha's approval, and he ordered the scribbler to think again. Next morning, the historian appeared before him, his eyes bloodshot from the sleepless night he had spent, and read him out his new description. High mountains, he declaimed, that reached even higher than crows can fly; the devil himself could barely climb up them, the demon would rip his sandals on their rocks, and even hens had to have their claws shod with iron to scale them.

The Pasha had found these images pleasing. The march was now over, night had fallen, and he tried to recall the phrases used, but he was tired and his weary mind could think of nothing but rest. It had been the longest and most exhausting expedition of his soldiering life. The ancient road, which was impassable in several places and which his engineers had repaired as fast as they could, bore the strange name of Egnatia. It went back to Roman times, but seemed to go on for ever. Sometimes, in the narrow gorges, his troops had stayed stuck until sappers cut a detour. Then the road became passable once more, and his army resumed its slow and dusty advance, as it had on the first, third, fifth and eighth day prior. Even now, when it was all over, that thick and unpleasant layer of grey dust still hung over his memory.

He heard horses neigh behind him. The closed carriage which had brought four women from his harem was still there, parked beside his tent.

Before leaving he had wondered several times whether he should bring his wives with him. Some of his friends had advised against it. It was a well-known fact, they said, that women bring ill fortune to a military campaign. Others took the opposite view and said that he should take them with him if he wanted to feel calm and relaxed and to sleep well (insofar as anyone can sleep well during war). Usually pashas did not take women with them in similar circumstances. But this expedition aimed to reach a very distant land; in addition, according to all forecasts, the siege was likely to last a long time. But those weren't the real reasons, because on all campaigns, however far-flung or long-drawn-out they might be, captives were always taken, and women won at the cost of soldiers' blood were indisputably more alluring than any member of a harem. However, friends had warned him that where he was going it would be difficult to take any female prisoners. The girls there were certainly very beautiful, but in the words of a poet who had accompanied an earlier raid into those lands, they were also as enticing and, alas! as unattainable as a dream. To escape from pursuit they would often throw themselves off a cliff. That's just poetic licence, some said, but the Pasha's closest friends shook their heads to say it was no such thing. In the end, as he was taking his leave, the Grand Vizier had noticed the small carriage with barred windows, and asked him why he was taking women to a land famed for the beauty of its own. Avoiding the Vizier's sly glance, he replied that he didn't want to have any share in the prisoners his valiant soldiers would take by their own efforts and blood.

During the march he hadn't had a thought for his wives. They must now surely be asleep in their lilac-coloured tent, worn out by the length of the journey.

Before feeling them on his own skin, he heard the raindrops falling on the tent. Then, after a short while, from somewhere inside the camp there rose the familiar sound of the rain drum. Its ominous roll, so different from the banging of heavy crates or the blare of the trumpets of war, summoned up the image of his soldiers who, despite their exhaustion, had to haul out the heavy tarpaulins to cover up the equipment, cursing at the weather as they laboured. He had heard it said that no foreign army except the Mongols had a special unit, as theirs did, whose job was to announce the coming of rain. Everything that's any use in the art of war, he said to himself, comes from the Mongols. Then he went inside his tent.

Orderlies had set up the Pasha's bed, placed the divans around it, and were now laying carpets on the floor. A strip of cloth embroidered with verses from the Koran had been hung at the entrance. Hooks had been hung in the customary manner from the top of the main pole so he could stow his scabbard and his cape. Contrary to what he had always expected, the more he rose in rank, the more gloomy his tent became.

He sat down on one of the divans and put his head between his hands as he waited for his chef-de-camp to finish his report. Almost all troops had now arrived, they had been allocated their proper camping places, guards, sentries and scouts had been posted all around – in sum, everything necessary had been done and was in order. The commander-in-chief could sleep peacefully.

The Pasha listened without interrupting. He didn't even take his head out of his hands, so that the chef-de-camp couldn't see his eyes, but only the ruby on his commander's middle finger. It was a ruby of the kind that because of its hue is called a bloodstone.

When his subaltern had left, Tursun Pasha stood up

and went out once again. The rain was lighter than he had thought it was from the noise it made inside the tent. His ears were still ringing with the chef-de-camp's litany of guards, sentries and scouts, but instead of calming him down, it had made him even more agitated. Night always bears a litter, he thought. He had heard the saying somewhere or other in his youth, but only when he was much older had he discovered that it did not refer to the consequences of love or lust, but to nasty surprises.

The night was pregnant and he was in its belly, all alone. He could see a faint glow leaking out of tents to the right of his own. Others were still awake, as he was. Maybe they were quartermasters, or exorcists or sorcerers warding off evil spirits. Normally, the astrologer, the chronicler, the spell-caster, the exorcists and the dream-interpreters had tents set next to each other. All of them knew more than he did about what lay in store, that was certain. Nevertheless, he did not trust them entirely.

The patter of raindrops was getting louder. The Pasha felt he was quite close to the sky and separated from it only by the feeble crown of his tent. A strange nostalgia overcame him as he thought of his bedroom at home, in his palace, where you could barely hear the sound of bad weather. He was usually more prone to longing for war. At home, lying in a room soundproofed by carpets, he would think eagerly of his campaign tent with the wind howling around it . . . Had he not now reached the age when he should don his slippers and retire to his peaceful Anatolian home? Should he not let go before the fall?

He knew it was not a practicable proposition. He was still young, but that was not the main reason. He had attained a rank where it was impossible to stand still. He was condemned either to rise even higher, or else to fall. The Empire was growing by the day. Whoever could prove himself the most energetic and courageous could have it all. Thousands of ambitious men were clawing their way like wild beasts towards wealth and fame. They were shoving others aside, often by intelligent manoeuvring, but even more often by plot and by poison.

He had recently felt the ground shifting under his own feet. There was no obvious cause for that uncertain sensation, which made it all the less easy to deal with. Like one of those mysterious diseases no one knows how to cure.

He had used all the means at his disposal to find out which hidden circles were plotting against him. A waste of time. He had not uncovered anything at all. His friends had begun to look at him pityingly. Especially after receiving his latest gift from the Sultan – a collection of armour. Everybody knew it was a bad omen. People were expecting him to fall, when, all of a sudden, news went round that he had been appointed commander of a huge expedition due to set off in short order against the Albanians. People said he must have still had some friends in high places, even if he had enemies aplenty. At the same time, however, it was clear that by sending him off to fight Skanderbeg, the Sultan was giving him one last chance.

It wasn't the first time the Padishah had acted in that way. He always appointed men who were playing their last card to head the most hazardous expeditions, well aware that the fiercest of warriors are those with their backs to the wall.

The Pasha rose and began to pace up and down on the plush carpet of his tent. Then he sat down again and took a thick swatch of papers and cardboard from a large leather satchel. Among the documents was the map of the fortress. The Pasha put it on his lap and pored over it. It contained very full details of the location and especially the height of the ramparts and the towers, the slope of the ground on every side, the specifications of the main door and of the secondary entrance to the south-west, the gully on the west side, and the river. The draftsman had put question marks in red ink in three or four places to mark the probable locations where the aqueduct entered and left the fortress. The Pasha stared fixedly at these marks.

One of his orderlies brought him his dinner on a tray, but he didn't touch it. His fingers ran through his worry-beads but the faint noise they made did no more than the patter of raindrops to dissipate the feeling of emptiness inside him.

He clapped his hands, and a eunuch appeared at the tent door.

"Bring me Exher," he said without even looking at the man.

The eunuch bowed to the ground but stayed where he was. He seemed to have something to say, but was too scared to open his mouth.

"What is it?" the Pasha asked, seeing the man was still there.

The eunuch mouthed something but made no sound.

"Is she ill?" the Pasha asked.

"No, Pasha, but you know that the hammam . . . and perhaps she . . ."

The Pasha motioned him to keep quiet. He looked at his beads once again. The night was going to be as long as a winter night.

"Bring her to me all the same," he blurted out.

The eunuch bowed again and then vanished like a shadow.

He came back a few moments later holding a young woman by the hand. Her hair had been done up in haste and she looked as if she was still asleep. She was the youngest of the women in his harem. Nobody knew her age, and nor did she. She couldn't have been more than sixteen.

The Pasha motioned to her. She sat on the bed. She did not arouse him one bit, but he lay down beside her nonetheless. She apologised for not having been able to perform her ablutions that night, for reasons beyond her control. The Pasha grasped that the sentence had been put in her mouth by the eunuch. He didn't answer. As he smelled the familiar perfume of the girl, which for the first time was blended with the smell of dust, it occurred to him briefly that maybe he should not lay his hand on a woman on the night before a battle, but the thought left his mind as casually as it had come into it.

He gazed at her pubis and was almost surprised by the vigorous tuft that the eunuch had not had time to shave, as he usually did. With this shadow over her sexual organ, the girl looked slightly foreign, and all the more desirable for it. He often told himself that he should abstain from making love when an affair of State was on his mind, but swung just as often to the opposite view, that it would help him cope. On this night, he overcame his hesitation.

He opened her legs with a gentle touch and, contrary to habit, as if he were afraid of bruising his young wife, he penetrated her with similar tenderness. The unusual consideration he showed did not surprise him; he guessed vaguely that it was connected to the long journey the girl had put up with alongside his soldiers, which made her almost part of his army.

He moved clumsily, as if his desire lay outside of his body, and it was only when he felt his seed spurt from him into the girl's warm belly that he livened up. His pleasure was brief but intense and sharp, as if it were all concentrated in itself, like the trunk of a tree with no branches.

The girl realised he had made love without desire. As she ascribed his coldness to the black tufts of her pubic hair rather than to her not having been bathed beforehand, she apologised once again. He didn't respond. He propped himself on his elbow, leaned back on the cushions, and started counting out his beads again. With a blush in her cheeks and her head on the pillow, she marvelled at the harsh and rough-hewn face of the man to whom she belonged.

He forgot all about her. He reached over to the pile of documents and extracted the map of the fortress from it. He drew two signs on it, and then a third, in black ink. The girl raised herself on an elbow and with her beautiful eyes cast a quizzical glance at the paper and its multitude of strange marks. Her master's cold, grey eyes did not budge from it. She made a small movement, as carefully as she could, so as not to disturb him. However, when she shifted her elbow, which was going numb, the bed moved, and one of its heavy pendants almost fell on to the sketch. She held her breath – but he hadn't noticed a thing. He was completely absorbed by the map.

She looked alternately at the Pasha's face and at the marks he was making on the map. She was extremely curious, and just as bold, for she asked:

"Is that what war is, then?"

He looked up and stared at her, as if surprised to see her lying there, then turned away and went back to poring over the map.

He carried on marking up the map for a long time. When he turned around, she had fallen asleep. She was breathing deeply, with her lips half-parted. She looked even younger than her years.

Rain was still falling and drumming on the tent.

As the Pasha gazed at the eyelashes and pale long neck of his fourth wife, his mind went back – who knows why? – to the latrines that had been constructed at top speed. The first ditch would now be creeping up to the river, like a water-snake . . . He lifted the blanket and, against his normal practice, took a look at his partner's delta, with its lips still wet. He thought he might have impregnated her. In nine months' time, she might give him a son . . . Approaching sleep made his mind wander to the *matériel* that should by now be under the tarpaulins, to the sentries, tomorrow's meeting of the war council, and back again to that woman's belly where his son may just have been engendered. When he grew up, would he ever imagine he had been conceived in a campaign tent, in the pouring rain, at the foot of a sinister citadel, far beyond the setting sun . . . ? Maybe he too would become a soldier, and as he rose in rank, maybe his tent too would move two hundred, six hundred, twelve hundred paces from the ramparts . . . "Allah! Why hast Thou made us thus?" he sighed as his head nodded, as if over a bottomless pit.

Their white tents have surrounded our citadel in the shape of an immense crown. At dawn on the morning after their arrival, the plain looked as if it were covered by a thick layer of snow. You could see no ground, no grass, no rocks. We climbed up to the battlements to get a view of this wintry scene. That was when we realised what a huge conflict our Castrioti had entered into with Murad Han, the most powerful prince of the age.

Their camp stretches out as far as the eye can see. The ground has vanished from sight and our hearts sink. We are now alone with only the clouds for company, as it were, while at our feet, like some nightmare vision, a myriad tents are forging a new landscape, a nowhere world, so to speak.

From here you can see the pink pavilion of the commander-in-chief. The day before yesterday he sent a delegation to seek our surrender. They stated their conditions quite clearly: they would not touch any of us, they would let us leave the citadel with our arms and chattels, and we could go wherever we chose. In return all they wanted were the keys to the castle so they could take down the black bird-flag (which is what they call our eagle) from the tower where it flies, for in their view it offends the firmament. In its place they want to raise the true son of the heavenly world, the crescent.

That is what they have been doing everywhere in recent times: they pretend to be pursuing a symbol when their real aim is conquest. They kept the issue of religion to the end, since they were sure it would be their winning bid. Their chief pointed to the bell-tower and said that as far as the instrument of torture was concerned (that is what they call the Holy Cross), we could, if we wished, hang on to it, and also, obviously, keep our Christian faith. You'll renounce it yourselves in due course, he added, because no nation could possibly prefer martyrdom to the peace of Islam.

Our answer was short and firm: neither the eagle nor the cross would ever be removed from our firmament; they were the symbols and the fate we had elected, and we would remain faithful to them. And so that each of us may keep his own symbols and fate according to the dispositions of the Lord, they had no alternative but to leave.

They did not wait for the interpreter to translate our last words before rising hurriedly to their feet in fury. They called us blind, said they had parleyed enough already, and that it was now time for arms to speak. Then they hastened towards the rear gate, taking a path through the centre of the courtyard so as to show off their magnificent costumes.

CHAPTER TWO

Mevla Çelebi, the chronicler, halted at fifty paces from the Pasha's tent. He stared with interest at the members of the council going into the pavilion one by one. Before the tent stood a metal pole with a brass crescent – the imperial emblem – perched atop. As he gazed at the high-ranking officers he tried to summon up the adjectives he would use to describe them in his chronicle. But all he could find were a few weak words, most of which had been worn out by his predecessors. Moreover, if he set aside those he had to use for the commander-in-chief, there were precious few left, and he would have to take care not to use them up too quickly. It was as if he had in his fist a bunch of jewels which he would have to distribute parsimoniously among these countless combatants.

Kurdisxhi, the captain of the *akinxhis*, had hardly got off his horse. His big ruddy head seemed to be still asleep. After him came the captain of the janissaries, the old but still ferocious Tavxha Tokmakhan, whose short legs looked as if they had been broken and badly put back together again. The commander of the *azabs*, Kara-Mukbil, strode in together with the army Mufti and two provincial commanders, or sanxhakbeys. Then along came Aslanhan, Deli Burxhuba, Ullu Bekbey, Olça Karaduman, Hatai, Uç Kurtogmuz and Uç Tunxhkurt, Bakerhanbey, Tahanka the deaf-mute, and the Alaybey of the army. It occurred to Çelebi that he would have to mention in his chronicle every one of these famous captains whose names echoed with the clash of steel, wild beasts, the black dust of long marches, storms, lightning and other suchlike subjects of fear.

With the exceptions of the commander-in-chief and Kara-Mukbil, whose oval faces were agreeable to the eye, and also of the Alaybey who, like most officers of his army, was a fine figure of a man, all the leaders had features that seemed to have been designed solely in order to make it harder for him to write his chronicle. Traits unworthy of appearing in a battle epic automatically came into his mind: Olça Karaduman's sty, the Mufti's asthma, Uç Kurtogmuz's extra tooth, the chilblains of his namesake, Uç Tunxhkurt, and the humped backs, short necks, scarecrow arms and sciatic shoulders of many others, and especially the coarse hairs sticking out of Kurdisxhi's nose.

He was musing on those nasal hairs, for who knows what reason, when he heard someone calling his name.

"Greetings, Mevla Çelebi!"

The chronicler turned round and bowed obsequiously down to the ground. The man who had hailed him was the army's Quartermaster General. He was coming towards him accompanied by Engineer Saruxha, the famous caster of cannon. Pale of skin, with eyes that were bloodshot from many sleepless nights, the engineer was the only member of the council who wore a black cloak, which accorded well with the aura of mystery surrounding his work.

"What are you doing here?" the Quartermaster asked Çelebi.

"I am observing the members of our illustrious council," the chronicler replied in a pompous tone, as if to justify his presence.

The Quartermaster General smiled at him, and walked on with Saruxha towards the door of the tent where sentries stood guard like statues.

Feeling guilty once again for the thoughts he had just had, the chronicler watched the tall, slim figure of the Quartermaster General, whom he had got to know during the long march. Quite unusually, this time he gave an impression of haughtiness.

The last to turn up for the meeting was Giaour, the architect. Çelebi tracked him and was struck by how unnatural his gait appeared. Nobody rightly knew the origins or the nationality of the man who was acquainted with every secret of the structures of fortresses. He had no known family, which was not surprising for a foreigner, but he seemed doubly alone because of the way he spoke – in a peculiar kind of Turkish that few could fully understand. As his chin was smooth, many suspected he was really a woman, or at least half-man and half-woman – a hermaphrodite, as people say.

The architect went in last. The duty guards were the only people left outside, and they started playing dice. The chronicler was burning to know what was being said inside the tent. Now, if he had been appointed secretary to the council of war as well as campaign chronicler, he would have been in a position to know everything. It was normal for the same man to occupy both positions. He accounted for his own limited station in various ways, depending on his mood. Sometimes he thought they had done him a favour by not overloading him with work and thus allowing him to concentrate entirely on the chronicle, which was intended to be an immortal record of the campaign. But at other times, such as now, as he looked at the Pasha's pavilion from a distance, he guessed the real reason for his exclusion, and felt bitter and disappointed.

He was about to move off when he saw several council members emerge from the tent. The Quartermaster General was among them. He saw Çelebi and called out to him.

"Come on, Mevla, come for a walk, we'll be able to chat. The council is now going over the details of the attack and those of us not directly involved have been asked to leave."

"When will the assault begin?" Çelebi asked shyly.

"In a week, I think. As soon as the two big cannon have been cast."

They sauntered slowly, with the Quartermaster's orderly following them like a shadow.

"Let's go into my tent for a drink and escape from all this racket," the Quartermaster said, making a wide gesture with his arm.

Çelebi put his hand on his heart and bowed low once more.

"You do me great honour."

Being invited into the tent to talk about history and

philosophy once more, as he had done a few days ago, filled him with a joy that evaporated instantly at the fear of disappointing his eminent friend.

"My head's bursting," the high official said, "and I need some respite. I've still got a pile of things to settle."

The chronicler listened to him with a guilty air.

"It's very odd," the Quartermaster said. "You historians usually attribute all the glory of conquest to military leaders. But mark my words, Mevla, mark them well: after the commander-in-chief's, it's this here head," he said, tapping his forehead with his index finger, "that has more worries than any other."

Çelebi bowed in homage.

"Supplying food to an army is the key problem in war," the Quartermaster went on, in a tone close to irritation. "Anybody can wave a sword about, but keeping forty thousand men fed and watered in a foreign, unpopulated and uncultivated land, now that's a hard nut to crack."

"How very true," the chronicler commented.

"Shall I tell you a secret?" the Quartermaster said all of a sudden. "The army you can see camped all around you has got supplies for only fifteen days!"

Çelebi raised his eyebrows, but thought they were insufficiently bushy to give adequate expression to his amazement.

"According to the plan," the officer went on, "supply trains are supposed to leave Edirne every two weeks. Granted, but given the huge distance they have to cover, can I rely on them? Provisions . . . If you ever hear that I've gone out of my mind, you'll know why!"

The chronicler wanted to protest: Whatever are

you saying? He nodded his head, even raised his arms – but they seemed too short to say what he now wanted to say.

"So all the responsibility falls on our shoulders," the other man went on. "If the cooks come and say one fine day that they've nothing left to fill their pots, who is the Pasha going to call to order? Obviously not Kurdisxhi, nor old Tavxha, nor any other captain. Only me!" And he stuck a finger into his breast as if it was a dagger.

Çelebi's face, on which deference and attentiveness were painted like a mask, now also expressed commiseration, which wasn't difficult, seeing that in its normal state it was deeply lined and wrinkled.

The Quartermaster General's tent was pitched at the very heart of the camp so that as they drew nearer to it they were walking among throngs of soldiers. Some of them were sitting outside their tents undoing their packs, others were picking their fleas without the slightest embarrassment. Çelebi recalled that no chronicle ever mentioned the tying and untying of soldier's backpacks. As for flea hunting, that was never spoken of either.

"What about the *akinxhis?*" he enquired, trying to banish all reprehensible thoughts from his mind. "Aren't they going to be allowed to pillage in the environs?"

"Of course they are," the officer replied. "However, the booty they take usually covers less than a fifth of the needs of the troops. And only in the early stages of a siege."

"That's odd . . ." the chronicler opined.

"There's only one solution: Venice."

Çelebi started with surprise.

"The Sultan has made an agreement with the

Serenissima. Venetian merchants are supposed to supply us with food and *matériel*."

The chronicler was astounded, but nodded his head.

"I understand why you are amazed," the Quartermaster said. "You must find it bizarre that we accuse Skanderbeg of being in the pay of Westerners while we do deals with Venice behind Skanderbeg's back. If I were in your shoes, I admit I would find that shocking."

The Quartermaster General put a formal smile on his lips, but his eyes were not smiling at all.

"That's politics for you, Mevla!"

The chronicler lowered his head. It was his way of taking cover whenever a conversation wandered into dangerous terrain.

A long line of *azabs* went past, carrying rushes on their backs.

The Quartermaster watched them go by.

"That's what they use, I believe, to weave the screens the soldiers use to shield themselves from burning projectiles. Have you really never seen a siege before?"

The chronicler blushed and said, "I have not had that good fortune."

"Oh! It's an impressive sight."

"I can imagine."

"Believe me," the general said in a more informal way. "I've taken part in many sieges, but this," he waved towards the castle walls, "is where the most fearful carnage of our times will take place. And you surely know as well as I do that great massacres always give birth to great books." He took a deep breath. "You really do have an opportunity to write a thundering chronicle redolent with pitch and blood, and it will be utterly different from the graceful whines composed at the fireside by squealers who never went to war."

Çelebi blushed again as he recalled the opening of his chronicle. "One day, if you like, I could read you some passages from what I have written," he said. "I would like to hope they will not disappoint you."

"Accepted! You know how much I like history."

A squad of janissaries marched past noisily.

"They're in a good mood," the Quartermaster said. "Today is pay day."

Çelebi remembered that pay was also never mentioned in that kind of narrative.

Troopers were setting out some oval tents. Further off, carters were unloading beams and rushes beside a ditch that had just been dug. The camp looked less like military quarters than a construction site.

"Look, there are the old hags from Rumelia," the Quartermaster said.

The chronicler turned his head to the left, where he could see a score and more of old women in an enclosure; they were busying themselves with pots hung over a campfire.

"What are they cooking up?" Çelebi asked.

"Balms for wounds, especially burns."

The chronicler looked at the tanned, impassive and aged faces of the women.

"Our warriors are going to suffer horrible injuries," the Quartermaster said sadly. "But they don't yet know the real function of the Rumelian women. They're reputed to be witches."

Çelebi looked away so as not to see the soldiers picking out their fleas. Many of them were in fact sitting cross-legged so as to examine the corns on the soles of their feet.

"Their feet are sore from the long march," the Quartermaster said with sympathy. "I've still never read a historical work that even mentions soldiers' feet."

The chronicler was sorry to have displayed his distaste, but the harm was done now.

"In truth, the vast Empire of which we are all so proud was enlarged only by these blistered and torn feet," the officer said with a touch of grandiloquence. "A friend often said to me: I am willing to kneel and kiss these stinking feet."

The chronicler didn't know what to do with himself. Fortunately for him, they had just got to the Quartermaster General's tent.

"So here's my den," the general said in a different tone of voice. "Come in, Mevla Çelebi. Do you like pomegranate syrup? In such scorching weather there's nothing better than the juice of a pomegranate to cool you down. And then, a conversation with a friend on matters of high interest is like a violet blooming among thorns. Isn't that so, Çelebi?"

The chronicler's mind flashed back to the soldiers' blisters and filthy feet, but he soon took solace in the thought that man is so great that all can be permitted him.

"I am overwhelmed by the friendship you bestow on me, a mere chronicler."

"Not at all!" the Quartermaster interrupted. "Your trade is most honourable: you are a historian. Only the uneducated could fail to grant you their esteem. Now, my dear friend, are you going to read me a few passages from your work, as you promised?"

Çelebi would have blushed with contentment had he not been so scared. After the whole exchange of courtesies, the chronicler, who knew the start of his work by heart, began to recite slowly as follows:

"At the behest of the Padishah, master of the universe, to whom men and genies owe total obedience, a myriad harems were abandoned and the lions set forth for the land of the Shqipetars . . ."

The Quartermaster General explained that this overture was not entirely lacking in poetry, but he would have preferred the idea of abandoned harems to be linked to some more basic element of human life, something more vital to the economy, such as, for example, the plough or the vine. He added that a few figures would give it more substance.

At that moment the general's secretary appeared at the tent door. His master signalled to him to come nearer, and the servant whispered something in the general's ear. The Quartermaster said "yes" several times, and "no" an equal number of times.

"What were we saying?" he asked the chronicler as soon as the secretary had left. "Ah yes, figures! But you mustn't take too much notice of me on this issue, because I'm obsessed with numbers. All day long I do nothing but count and reckon!"

The secretary reappeared.

"A messenger from the Pasha," he blurted out as soon as he saw his master scowl.

The courier came close to the general, bent down to speak in his ear, and went on whispering in that position for a long while. Then he put his own ear to the Quartermaster's mouth to collect the reply.

"Let's go out," the Quartermaster suggested when the courier had left. "We'll have a better chance to talk outdoors. Otherwise the thorns of everyday business will throttle the violet of our conversation!"

Dusk was falling. The camp was in a state of lively activity. *Akinxhis* were coming from all directions, leading their horses to water. Standards rustled in the wind from the tips of the tent poles. With the addition of a handful of flowers to add their smell, the many-coloured camp would have looked less like a military installation than a blooming garden. The chronicler remembered that none of his colleagues had ever described an army as a flower garden – a *gulistan* – but that was what he was going to do. He would liken it to a meadow, or else to a polychrome kilim, but one from which, as soon as the order to move forward was given, would emerge the black fringes of death.

They had almost reached the centre-point of the camp when they ran into the engineer, Saruxha. He was wandering around looking absent-minded.

"Is the meeting over?" the Quartermaster General enquired.

"Yes, it's just ended. I'm dead tired," Saruxha replied, rubbing his red-rimmed eyes. "We've not had a wink of sleep for three nights in a row. Today the Pasha gave us final orders to ready the cannon for next week . . . In eight days, he said, he wants to hear their blast."

"Will you manage?"

"I don't know. We might. But you can't imagine how difficult the work will be. Especially as we're using a new kind of weapon, one which has never been made before, so I have to attend to every detail of manufacture."

"I understand," the Quartermaster said.

"Do you want to have a look at the foundry?" Saruxha asked, and, without waiting for an answer, he led them off across waste ground.

The chronicler was delighted to be given so much trust. Before leaving the capital he had heard all kinds of rumours about the new weapon. People spoke of it alternately with admiration and horror, as is normal with a secret weapon. They said its roar would make you deaf for the rest of your life, and its blast would topple everything around it within a radius of several leagues.

During the long march he had noticed the camels that were alleged to be carrying pieces of the barrel destined to serve the big cannon. The soldiers who marched silently alongside never took their eyes off the rain-soaked black tarpaulins hiding the mortal secret.

Çelebi itched to learn more about the camels' packs but he was frightened of arousing suspicion. When at last he overcame his shyness and questioned the Quartermaster, whom he had just got to know, the latter burst out laughing, with his hands on hips. Those heavy packs, he said, don't have any tubes in them at all. All that was in them were bars of iron and bronze, and a special kind of coal. "So you're going to ask me, where then is the secret weapon? I'll tell you, Mevla Çelebi. The big, fearsome cannon are in a tiny little satchel . . . as tiny as the one over my shoulder, here . . . Don't look at me like that, I'm not pulling your leg!" Now he whispered it into Mevla's ear, nodding towards a waxen-faced man wrapped in a black cloak: "The secret cannon really is in a satchel." It took the chronicler a little while to grasp that in that wan figure's shoulder bag were to be found secret designs and formulae that would be used for casting the big gun.

The foundry had been set up away from the camp in an area that was entirely fenced off and under heavy guard. It was separated from the stream by a hillock, and at twenty paces from the gate stood a sign saying: "Forbidden Zone".

"It's well guarded, day and night," the engineer said. "Spies might try to steal our secret."

The engineer acted as their tour guide through the long shack that had been thrown up and gave them copious explanations of what could be seen. The forge and the ovens had just been lit, and the flames gave off stifling heat. Shirtless, soot-blackened men dripping with sweat were busy at work.

Heaps of iron and bronze ingots and huge clay moulds covered most of the floor.

The engineer showed them the designs for the giant cannon.

The visitors looked with wonderment at the mass of straight lines, arcs and circles meticulously traced out on the blueprints.

"This one's the biggest," Saruxha said as he showed them one of the drawings. "My artificers have already dubbed it *balyemeztop*!"

"The gun that eats no honey? Why call it by such a strange name?" the Quartermaster asked.

"Because it prefers to eat men!" Saruxha replied. "It's a whimsical cannon, if I may say, a bit like a spoiled child who says to its mother one fine morning, 'I'm fed up with honey!' . . . Now come and see the place where it will be cast," he added as he moved off in another direction. "Here's the great hole where the clay moulds will be laid down, and over there are the six furnaces where the metal will be melted. A standard cannon takes one furnace, but for this one, six will barely suffice! That's one of the main secrets of the casting. All six furnaces have to produce molten metal at exactly the same degree of fusion at precisely the same time. If there's the tiniest crack, the tiniest bubble, so to speak, then the cannon will burst apart when it's fired."

The Quartermaster General gave a whistle of astonishment.

Although he too was amazed at what he had heard, Mevla Çelebi was sufficiently astute not to turn his head towards the general in case the latter, once he had regained his poise, might feel annoyed at having been caught in a moment of weakness by a mere chronicler, or, in other words, at having let himself be seen to be astonished, when he was supposed to be far above such emotions.

But the Quartermaster General wasn't trying to hide his bewilderment. The chronicler, for his part, trembled at the thought that Engineer Saruxha was engaged on God's work, or else the Devil's own, by having his furnaces produce a fiery liquid that Allah himself caused the earth to spew out through the mouths of volcanoes. Labour of that kind usually brought severe punishment.

As the engineer went on explaining how the casting

would be done, in their eyes he slowly turned into a wizard, wrapped in his black cloak, about to perform some ancient, mysterious ritual.

"It is the first time that cannon of this kind are to be used in the whole military history of humankind," Saruxha finally declared with pride. "An earthquake will sound like a lullaby next to their terrible thunder."

They looked at him with admiration.

"This is where the most modern war the world has ever known is about to be waged," he concluded, staring at the chronicler.

Çelebi was worried.

"The Padishah's priority at present is to force the Balkans into submission," the Quartermaster commented. "Obviously, he will spare no expense to achieve his aim."

"This is my right-hand man," Saruxha said as he turned towards a tall, pale and worn-out young man who was coming towards them.

The young man glanced nonchalantly at the visitors, made a gesture that could barely be understood as a greeting, and then whispered a few words in the engineer's ear.

"You're amazed I picked that lad as my first assistant, aren't you?" Saruxha asked when the youngster had walked off. "Most people share your view. He doesn't look the part, but he is extremely able."

They said nothing.

"In this shed we will cast four other, smaller cannon, but they will be no less fearsome than the big one," the engineer went on. "They are called mortars, and they shoot cannon-balls in a curved trajectory. Unlike cannon which hit the walls straight on, mortars can rain down on the castle's inner parts from above, like a calamity falling from the heavens."

He picked up a lump of coal and piece of board from the ground.

"Let's suppose this is the castle wall. We put the cannon here. Its shot takes a relatively straight path" – he drew a line – "and hits the wall here. But the shot from the mortar or bombard rises high in the sky, almost innocently, if I may say so, as if it had no intention of hitting the wall – and then falls almost vertically behind it." With his hand, which the chronicler thought he saw shaking a little, he made out the shape of the two arcs in the air. "Bombards make a noise that sounds like the moaning of a stormy sea."

"Allah!" the chronicler cried out.

"Where did you learn how to do all this?" the Quartermaster General asked.

The engineer looked at him evasively.

"From my master, Saruhanli. I was his first assistant."

"He's in prison now, isn't he?"

"Yes," Saruxha replied. "The Sultan had him put away in the fortress of Bogazkezen."

"And nobody knows why?" the chronicler ventured timidly.

"I know why," the engineer replied.

The Quartermaster General raised his eyes and glanced at Saruxha with surprise.

"Recently, the poor old man's mind began to wander. He refused to make cannon of larger calibre. He claimed it was impossible, but in fact, as he told me, he didn't want to do it. If we make them even bigger, he would say, then the cannon will become a terrible scourge that will decimate the human race. The monster has come into the world, he said by way of explanation, and we can't put it back where it came from. The best we can do is to keep its barrel no bigger than it is now. If we enlarge it further, the cannon will devour the world. The old man stopped experimenting. That's why the Sultan had him arrested."

The engineer picked up a piece of clay and rubbed it until it turned to dust, and said, "That's what's happened to him."

The other two men nodded.

"But I have a different view of the matter," the engineer explained. "I think that if we give in to scruples of that kind, then science will come to a halt. War or no war, science must advance. I don't really mind who uses this weapon, or against whom it is used. What matters to me is that it should hurl a cannon-ball along a path identical to my calculation of the trajectory. The rest of it is your business." And on that abrupt note, he stopped.

"I've been given to understand that the money for making this weapon was donated by one of the Sultan's wives for the salvation of her soul," the Quartermaster General said, obviously intending to change the topic of conversation.

"For the salvation of her soul?" Çelebi asked, thinking the detail worthy of figuring in his chronicle. "Is it expensive?" he added after a pause, astounded at his own temerity.

"He's the one to know," the engineer said, pointing at the Quartermaster. "All I can tell you about is the gun's range and firepower."

The chronicler smiled.

"Oh yes, the big gun costs a lot of money," the Quartermaster said. "A very great deal. Especially now that we are at war, and the price of bronze has soared."

He narrowed his eyes and made a quick mental calculation.

"Two million silver aspers," he blurted out.

The chronicler was awe-struck. But the figure made no impact whatever on the master caster.

"To pay that much for the salvation of one's soul may seem prohibitively expensive," the Quartermaster said, "but if the cannon-balls break through those ramparts in a few days' time, they'll be worth their weight in gold."

An ironical smile hovered over his face.

"At the siege of Trabzon," he continued, "when the first cannon, which was much smaller than this one, shot its first ball, many of those present thought the barrel had grunted 'Allah!'. But what I thought I heard through the roar, maybe because I think about it all the time, was the word 'Taxation!'"

Once again the chronicler was struck dumb. The engineer, for his part, started to laugh out loud.

"You don't realise the full meaning of that word, nor how many things, including the siege of this fortress, depend on it," the Quartermaster observed.

"Well, when the gun fires," the engineer said, "I don't hear it say 'Allah!' or 'Taxation' at all. All I think about is that the power and noise of the explosion are the product of the amount of gunpowder packed behind the cannon-ball combined with the precise diameter and length of the barrel."

The Quartermaster General smiled. Çelebi, for his

part, pondered on his having become friendly with powerful and learned men, and wondered how long he could keep up conversations of this kind, which rose into spheres he had never previously encountered.

"Let's go outside for a breath of air," the Quarter-master suggested.

Saruxha walked with them as far as the door.

"People say that these new weapons will change the nature of war," the chronicler said. "That they'll make citadels redundant."

Saruxha shook his head doubtfully.

"Indeed they might. People also say they will make other weapons obsolete."

"Who are the 'people' saying these things?" the Quartermaster butted in. "You don't believe these cannon can overcome the fortress all by themselves, do you?"

"I certainly wish they could," Saruxha replied, "because they are, at bottom, my creations. However, I take a rather different view. I think that although the guns will play a role in the victory, what really matter are the soldiers of our great Padishah. It is they who will storm the fortress."

"Quite right," the Quartermaster General said.

"The cannon will have at least one other effect," Saruxha added. "Their thunderous noise will spread panic among the besieged and break their courage. That's a considerable help, isn't it?"

"It's very important," the Quartermaster agreed. "And I'm not thinking only of those wretches. The whole of Christendom trembles when it hears speak of our new weapon. It has already become a legend."

"I would walk with you for a while," Saruxha said, "but this evening I've still got a thousand things to do. Casting should begin around midnight."

"Don't apologise, and thank you," the visitors replied almost in unison.

Meanwhile night had fallen and fires had been lit here and there around the camp. Beside one of them, somewhere out there in the dark, someone was singing a slow and sorrowful chant. Further off, two ragged dervishes were mumbling their prayers.

They walked on in silence. The chronicler thought how strange it was that men of such different kinds should all be serving the Padishah, brought together by war in this god-forsaken spot at the end of the world.

They could still hear chanting in the far distance, and could just about make out the refrain: "O Fate, O Fate . . ."